THE MUTANT WEAPON

by

Murray Leinster

BORGO PRESS / WILDSIDE PRESS

www.wildsidepress.com

THE MUTANT WEAPON

Copyright ©, 1959, by Ace Books, Inc.

THE SPACE DOCTOR'S DILEMMA

The only links between the far-flung colonies through-out the galaxy were the Medical Service spaceships. It was natural therefore that when these lonely travelers. paid a call, they were given a royal welcome.

No wonder Med Serviceman Calhoun got the shock of his life when the landing grid on newly colonized Maris III tried to destroy his ship!

And when he managed to make a crash-landing, he was even more shocked by the grisly fact that most of the colonists had starved to death — even though there was plenty of food around. Forgetting his horror, Calhoun had to move fast to keep the fate of Maris III from being the beginning of the end for all the colonial planets.

THE AUTHOR

Will F. Jenkins, better known to readers under his popular pen-name of *Murray Leinster,* has been entertaining the public with his exciting fiction for several decades. Called the dean of modern science-fiction, he was writing these amazing super-science adventures back in the early twenties before there ever was such a thing as an all-fantasy magazine. His short stories, novelettes, and serial novels have appeared in most ·of the major American magazines, both slick and pulp, and many have been reprinted all over the world. He has made a distinguished name for himself (or rather two names!) in the fields of adventure, historical, western, sea and suspense stories.

Ace Books have published the following Murray Leinster novels: GATEWAY TO ELSEWHERE (D-53), THE BRAIN-STEALERS (D-79), THE OTHER SIDE OF HERE (D-94), THE FORGOTTEN PLANET (D-146), and CITY ON THE MOON (D-277).

CHAPTER I

"The probability of unfavorable consequences cannot be zero in any action of common life, but the probability increases by a very high power as a series of actions is lengthened. The effect of moral considerations, in conduct, may be stated to be a mathematically verifiable reduction in the number of unfavorable possible chance happenings. Of course, whether this process is called the intelligent use of probability, or ethics, or piety, makes no difference in the facts. It is the method by which unfavorable chance happenings are made least probable. Arbitrary actions such as we call criminal cannot ever be justified by mathematics. For example . . ."

Probability and Human Conduct——Fitzgerald

CALHOUN lay in his bunk and read Fitzgerald on *Probability and Human Conduct* as the little Med Ship floated in overdrive. In overdrive travel there is nothing to do but pass the time away. Murgatroyd, the *tormal*, slept curled up in a ball in one corner of the small ship's cabin. His tail was meticulously curled about his nose. The ship's lights burned steadily. There were those small random noises which have to be provided to keep a man sane in the dead stillness of a ship traveling at very many times the speed of light. Calhoun turned a page and yawned.

Something stirred somewhere. There was a click, and a taped voice said:

"When the tone sounds, breakout will be five seconds off."

A metronomic clicking, grave and deliberate, resounded in the stillness. Calhoun heaved himself up from the bunk and marked his place in the book. He moved to and seated himself in the control chair and fastened the safety belt. He said:

"Murgatroyd. Hark, hark the lark in Heaven's something-or-other doth sing. Wake up and comb your whiskers. We're getting there."

Murgatroyd opened one eye and saw Calhoun in the pilot's chair. He uncurled himself and padded to a place where there was something to grab hold of. He regarded Calhoun with bright eyes.

"*Bong!*" said the tape. It counted down. "Five . . . four . . . three . . . two . . one . . ."

It stopped. The ship popped out of overdrive. The sensation was unmistakable. Calhoun's stomach seemed to turn over twice, and he had a sickish feeling of spiraling dizzily in what was somehow a cone. He swallowed. Murgatroyd made gulping noises. Outside, everything changed.

The sun Maris blazed silently in emptiness off to port. The Cetis star-cluster was astern, and the light by which it could be seen had traveled for many years to reach here, though Calhoun had left Med Headquarters only three weeks before. The third planet of Maris swung splendidly in its orbit. Calhoun checked, and nodded in satisfaction. He spoke over his shoulder to Murgatroyd.

"We're here, all right."

"*Chee!*" shrilled Murgatroyd.

He uncoiled his tail from about a cabinet handle and hopped up to look at the vision screen. What he saw, of course, meant nothing to him. But all *tormals* imitate the actions of human beings, as parrots imitate their speech. He blinked wisely at the screen and turned his eyes to Calhoun.

"It's Maris III," Calhoun told him, "and pretty close. It's a colony of Dettra Two. One city was reported started two Earth-years ago. It should just about be colonized now."

"*Chee-chee!*" shrilled Murgatroyd.

"So get out of the way," commanded Calhoun. "We'll make our approach and I'll tell 'em we're here."

He made a standard approach on interplanetary drive. Naturally, it was a long process: But after some hours he flipped over the call switch and made the usual identification and landing request.

"Med Ship Aesclipus Twenty to ground," he said into the transmitter. "Requesting co-ordinates for landing. Our mass is fifty tons. Repeat, five-oh tons. Purpose of landing: planetary health inspection."

He relaxed. This job ought to be purest routine. There was a landing grid in the spaceport city on Maris III. From its control room instructions should be sent, indicating a position some five planetary diameters from the surface of that world. Calhoun's little ship should repair to that spot. The giant landing grid should then reach out its specialized force field, lock onto the ship, and bring it gently but irresistibly down to ground. Then Calhoun, representing Med Service, should confer gravely with planetary authorities about public health conditions on Maris III.

It was not to be expected that anything important would turn up. Calhoun would deliver full details of recent advances in the science of medicine. These might already have reached Maris III in the ordinary course of commerce, but he would make sure. He might—but it was unlikely—learn of some novelty worked out here. In any case, within three days he should return to the small Med Ship, the landing grid should heave it firmly heavenward to not less than five planetary diameters distance, and there release it. And Calhoun and Murgatroyd and the Med Ship should flick into overdrive and speed back toward headquarters, from whence they had come.

Right now, Calhoun waited for an answer to his landing call. But he regarded the vast disk of the nearby planet.

"By the map," he observed to Murgatroyd, "the city ought to be on shore of that bay somewhere near the terminus. Close to the sunset line."

His call was answered. A voice said incredulously on the spacephone speaker:

"What? What's that? What's that you say?"

"Med Ship Aesclipus Twenty," Calhoun repeated patiently. "Requesting co-ordinates for landing. Our mass is fifty tons. Repeat, five-oh tons. Purpose of landing: planetary health inspection."

The voice said more incredulously still:

"A Med Ship? Holy—" By the change of sound, the man

down on the planet had turned away from the microphone. *"Hey! Listen to this!"*

There was abrupt silence. Calhoun raised his eyebrows. He drummed on the control desk before him. There was a long pause. A very long pause. Then a new voice came on the spacephone, up from the ground:

"You up there! Identify yourself!"

Calhoun said very politely:

"This is Med Ship Aesclipus Twenty. I would like to come to ground. Purpose of landing: health inspection."

"Wait," said the voice from the planet. It sounded strained.

A murmuring sounded, transmitted from fifty thousand miles away. Then there was a click. The transmitter down below had cut off. Calhoun raised his eyebrows again. This was not according to routine. Not at all! The Med Service was badly overworked and understaffed. The resources of interplanetary services were always apt to be stretched to their utmost, because there could be no galactic government as such. Many thousands of occupied planets, the closest of them light-years apart, couldn't hold elections or have political parties for the simple reason that travel, even in overdrive, was too slow. They could only have service organizations whose authority depended on the consent of the people served, and whose support had to be gathered when and as it was possible.

But the Med Service was admittedly important. The local Sector Headquarters was in the Cetis cluster. It was a sort of interstellar clinic, with additions. It gathered and disseminated the results of experience in health and medicine among some thousands of colony-worlds, and from time to time it made contact with other headquarters carrying on the same work elsewhere. It admittedly took fifty years for a new technique in gene selection to cross the occupied part of the galaxy, but it was a three-year voyage in overdrive to cover the same distance direct. And the Med Service was worthwhile. There was no problem of human ecological adjustment it had so far been unable to solve, and there were some dozens of planets whose human colonies

owed their existence to it. There was nowhere, nowhere at
at all, that a Med Ship was not welcomed on its errand
from headquarters.

"Aground there!" said Calhoun sharply. "What's the matter?
Are you landing me or not?"

There was no answer. Then, suddenly, every sound-pro-
ducing device in the ship abruptly emitted a hoarse and
monstrous noise. The lights flashed up and circuit breakers
cut them off. The nearest-object horn squawked. The hull-
temperature warning squealed. The ship's internal gravity
field tugged horribly for an instant and went off. Every
device within the ship designed to notify emergency clanged
or shrieked or roared or screamed. There was a momentary
bedlam.

It lasted for part of a second only. Then everything stopped.
There was no weight within the ship, and there were no
lights. There was dead silence, and Murgatroyd made whim-
pering sounds in the darkness.

Calhoun thought absurdly to himself, *According to the
book, this is an unfavorable chance consequence of something or other.* But it was more than an unfavorable chance
occurrence. It was an intentional and drastic and possibly a
deadly one.

"Somebody's acting up," said Calhoun measuredly, in the
blackness. "What the hell's the matter with them?"

He flipped the screen switch to bring back vision of what
was outside. The vision screens of a ship are very carefully
fused against overload burnouts, because there is nothing
in all the cosmos quite as helpless and foredoomed as a
ship which is blind in the emptiness of space. But the screens
did not light again. They couldn't. The cutouts hadn't worked
in time.

Calhoun's scalp crawled. But as his eyes adjusted, he saw
the pale fluorescent handles of switches and doors. They
hadn't been made fluorescent in expectation of an emergency
like this, of course, but they would help a great deal. He
knew what had happened. It could only be one thing—a
landing-grid field clamped on the fifty-ton Med Ship with
the power needed to grasp and land a twenty-thousand-ton

liner. At that strength it would paralyze every instrument and blow every cutoff. It could not be accidental. The reception of the news of his identity, the repeated request that he identify himself, and then the demand that he wait . . . This murderous performance was deliberate.

"Maybe," said Calhoun in the inky-black cabin, "as a Med Ship our arrival is an unfavorable chance consequence of something—and somebody means to keep us from happening. It looks like it."

Murgatroyd whimpered.

"And I think," added Calhoun coldly, "that somebody may need a swift kick in the negative feedback!"

He released himself from the safety belt and dived across the cabin in which there was now no weight at all. In the blackness he opened a cabinet door. What he did inside was customarily done by a man wearing thick insulated gloves, in the landing grid back at headquarters. He threw certain switches which would allow the discharge of the power-storage cells which worked the Med Ship's overdrive. Monstrous quantities of energy were required to put even a fifty-ton ship into overdrive, and monstrous amounts were returned when it came out. The power amounted to ounces of pure, raw energy, and as a safety precaution such amounts were normally put into the Duhanne cells only just before a Med Ship's launching, and drained out again on its return. But now, Calhoun threw switches which made a rather incredible amount of power available for dumping into the landing-grid field about him— if necessary.

He floated back to the control chair.

The ship lurched. Violently. It was being moved by the grid field without any gentleness at all. Calhoun's hands barely grasped the back of his pilot's chair before the jerk came, and it almost tore them free. He just missed being flung against the back of the cabin by the applied acceleration. But he was a long way out from the planet. He was at the end of a lever fifty thousand miles long, and for that lever to be used to shake him too brutally would require special adjustments. But somebody was making them. The jerk reversed directions. He was flung savagely against the

chair to which he'd been clinging. He struggled. Another
yank, in another direction. Another one still. It flung him
violently into the chair.

Behind him, Murgatroyd squealed angrily as he went
hurtling across the cabin. He grabbed for holding places with
all four paws and his tail.

Another shake. Calhoun had barely fastened the safety
belt before a furious jolt nearly flung him out of it again
to crash against the cabin ceiling. Still another vicious surge
of acceleration, and he scrabbled for the controls. The yank-
ing and plunging of the ship increased intolerably. He was
nauseated. Once he was thrust so furiously into the control
chair that the was on the verge of blacking out; and then
the direction of thrust was changed to the exact opposite
so that the blood rushing to his head seemed about to
explode it. His arms flailed out of control. He became dazed.
But when his hands were flung against the control board, he
tried, despite their bruising, to cling to the control-knobs,
and each time he threw them over. Practically all his circuits were blown, but there was one—

His numbing fingers threw it. There was a roar so fierce
that it seemed to be an explosion. He'd reached the switch
which made effective the discharge circuit of his Duhanne
cells. He'd thrown it. It was designed to let the little ship's
overdrive power reserve flow into storage at headquarters
on return from duty. Now, though, it poured into the landing field outside. It amounted to hundreds of millions of
kilowatt hours, delivered in the fraction of a second. There
was the smell of ozone. The sound was like a thunderclap.

But abruptly there was a strange and incredible peace.
The lights came on waveringly as his shaking fingers restored the circuit breakers. Murgatroyd shrilled indignantly,
clinging desperately to an instrument rack. But the vision
screens did not light again. Calhoun swore. Swiftly, he threw
more circuit restorers. The nearest-object indicator told of the
presence of Maris III at forty-odd thousand miles. The hull-
temperature indicator was up some fifty-six degrees. The
internal-gravity field came on faintly, and then built up to
normal. But the screens would not light. They were per-

manently dead. Calhoun raged for seconds. Then he got hold of himself.

"*Chee-chee-chee!*" chattered Murgatroyd desperately. "*Chee-chee!*"

"Shut up!" growled Calhoun. "Some bright lad aground thought up a new way to commit murder. Damned near got away with it, too! He figured he'd shake us to death like a dog does a rat, only he was using a landing-grid field to do it with. Right now, I hope I fried him!"

But it was not likely. Such quantities of power as are used to handle twenty-thousand-ton spaceliners are not controlled direct, but by relays. The power Calhoun had flung into the grid field should have blown out the grid's transformers with a spectacular display of fireworks, but it was hardly probable it had gotten back to the individual at the controls.

"But I suspect," observed Calhoun vengefully, "that he'll consider this business an unfavorable occurrence. Somebody'll twist his tail too, either for trying what he did or for not getting away with it! Only, as a matter of pure precaution—

His expression changed suddenly. He'd been trying not to think of the consequences of having no sight of the cosmos outside the ship. Now he remembered the electron telescope. It had not been in circuit, so it could not have been burned out like his vision screens. He switched it on. A star-field appeared over his head.

"*Chee-chee!*" cried Murgatroyd hysterically.

Calhoun glanced at him. The jerking of the ship had shifted the instruments in the rack to which Murgatroyd clung. Clipped into place though they were, they'd caught Murgatroyd's tail and pinched it tightly.

"You'll have to wait," snapped Calhoun. "Right now I've got to make us look like a successful accident. Otherwise, whoever tried to spread us all over the cabin walls will try something else!"

The Med Ship flung through space in whatever direction and at whatever velocity it had possessed when the grid field blew. Calhoun shifted the electron-telescope field and simultaneously threw on the emergency rocket controls. There was a growling of the pencil-thin, high-velocity blasts. There was a surging of the ship.

"No straight-line stuff," Calhoun reminded himself.

He swung the ship into a dizzy spiral, as if innumerable things had been torn or battered loose in the ship and its rockets had come on of themselves. Painstakingly, he jettisoned in one explosive burst all the stored waste of his journey which could not be disposed of while in overdrive. To any space-scanning instrument on the ground, it would look like something detonating violently inside the ship.

"Now—"

The planet Marris III swung across the electron telescope's field. It looked hideously near, but that was the telescope's magnification. Yet Calhoun sweated. He looked at the nearest-object dial for reassurance. The planet was nearer by a thousand miles.

"Hah!" said Calhoun.

He changed the ship's spiral course. He changed it again. He abruptly reversed the direction of its turn. Adequate training in space combat could have helped plot an evasion course, but it might have been recognizable. Nobody could anticipate his maneuvers now, though. He adjusted the telescope next time the planet swept across its field, and flipped on the photorecorder. Then he pulled out of the spiral, whirled the ship until the city was covered by the telescope, and ran the recorder as long as he dared keep a straight course. Then he swooped toward the planet in a crazy, twisting fall with erratic intermissions, and made a final lunatic dash almost parallel to the planet's surface.

At five hundred miles he unshielded the ports, which of necessity had to be kept covered in clear space. There was a sky which was vividly bright with stars. There was a vast blackness off to starboard which was the night side of the planet.

He went down. At four hundred miles the outside-pressure indicator wavered away from its pin. He used it like a Pilot-tube recording, doing sums in his head to figure the static pressure that should exist at this height, to compare with the dynamic pressure produced by his velocity through the near hard vacuum. The pressure should have been substantially zero. He swung the ship end-for-end and killed velocity to bring the pressure indication down. The ship descended. Two hundred miles. He saw the thin bright line of sunshine at the limb of the planet. Down to one hundred. He cut the rockets and let the ship fall silently, swinging its nose up.

At ten miles he listened for man-made radiation. There was nothing in the electromagnetic spectrum but the crackling of static in an electric storm which might be a thousand miles away. At five miles height the nearest-object indicator, near the bottom of its scale, wavered in a fashion to prove that he was still moving laterally across mountainous country. He swung the ship and killed that velocity too.

At two miles he used the rockets for deceleration. The pencil-thin flame reached down for an incredible distance. By naked-eye observation out a port, he tilted the fiercely roaring, swiftly falling ship until hillsides and forests underneath him ceased to move. By that time he was very low indeed.

He reached ground on a mountainside which was lighted by the blue-white flame of the rocket blast. He chose an area in which the treetops were almost flat, indicating something like a plateau underneath. Murgatroyd was practically frantic by this time because of his capture and the pinching of his tail, but Calhoun could not spare time to release him. He let the ship down gently, gently, trying to descend in an absolutely vertical line.

If he didn't do it perfectly, he came very close. The ship settled into what was practically a burned-away tunnel among monstrous trees. The slender, high-velocity flame did not splash when it reached ground. It penetrated. It burned a hole for itself through humus and clay and bedrock. When the ship touched and settled, there was boiling molten stone some sixty feet underground; but there was only a small scratching sound as it came to rest. A flame-amputated tree limb rubbed tentatively against the hull.

Calhoun turned off the rockets. The ship swayed slightly

and there were crunching noises. Then it was still on its landing fins.

"Now," said Calhoun, "I can take care of you, Murgatroyd."

He flicked on the switches of the exterior microphones, which were much more sensitive than human ears. The radiation detectors were still in action. They reported only the cracklings of the distant storm.

But the microphones brought in the moaning of wind over nearby mountaintops, and the almost deafening susurrus of rustling leaves. Underneath these noises there was a bedlam of other natural sounds. There were chirpings and hootings and squeaks, and the gruntings made by native animal life. These sounds had a singularly peaceful quality. When Calhoun toned them down to be no more than background noise, they suggested the sort of concert of night-creatures which to men has always seemed an indication of purest tranquility.

Presently Calhoun looked at the pictures the photorecorder had taken while the telescope's field swept over the city. It was the colony-city reported to have been begun two years before, to receive colonists from Dettra Two. It was the city of the landing-grid which had tried to destroy the Med Ship as a dog kills a rat, by shaking it to fragments, some forty thousand miles in space. It was the city which had made Calhoun land with his vision plates blinded; which had made him pretend his ship was internally a wreck; which had drained his power reserves of some hundreds of millions of kilowatt-hours of energy. It was the city which had made his return to Med Headquarters impossible.

He inspected the telescopic pictures. They were very clear. They showed the city with astonishing detail. There was a lacy pattern of highways, with their medallions of multiple-dwelling units. There were the lavish park areas between the buildings of this planetary capital. There was the landing grid itself, a half-mile high structure of steel girders, a full mile in diameter.

But there were no vehicles on the highways. There were no specks on the overpasses to indicate people on foot. There were no 'copters on the building roofs, nor were there objects in mid-air to tell of air traffic.

The city was either deserted or it had never been occupied. But it was absolutely intact. The structures were perfect. There was no indication of past panic or disaster, and even the highways had not been overgrown by vegetation. But it was empty—or else it was dead.

But somebody in it had tried very ferociously and with singular effectiveness to try to destroy the Med Ship.

Because it was a Med Ship.

Calhoun raised his eyebrows and looked at Murgatroyd. "Why is all this?" he asked. "Have you any ideas?"

"*Chee!*" shrilled Murgatroyd.

CHAPTER II

"The purpose of a contemplated human action is always the attainment of a desired subjective experience. But a subjective experience is desired both in terms of intensity and of duration. For an individual the temptingness of different degrees of intensity of experience is readily computed. However, the temptingness of different durations is equally necessary for an estimate of the probability of a given person performing a given action. This modification of desirability by expected duration depends on the individual's time sense; its acuity and its accuracy. Measurements of time sense . . ."

Probability and Human Conduct——Fitzgerald

EVENTUALLY Calhoun left the ship and found a cultivated field and a dead man and other things. But while in the Med Ship he found only bewilderment. The first morning he carefully monitored the entire communications spectrum. There were no man-made signals in the air of Maris III. That was proof the world was uninhabited. But the ship's external microphones picked up a rocket roar in mid-morning. Calhoun looked, and saw the faint white trail of the rocket against the blue of the sky. The fact that he saw it was proof that it was in atmosphere. And that was evidence that the rocket was taking photographs for signs of the crater the Med Ship should have made in a crash landing.

The fact of search was proof that the planet was inhabited, but the silence of the radio spectrum said that it wasn't. The absence of traffic in the city said that it was dead or empty, but there were people there because they'd answered Calhoun's hail, and tried to kill him when he identified himself. But nobody would want to destroy a Med Ship except to prevent a health inspection, and nobody would want to prevent an inspection unless there was a situation aground that the Med Service ought to know about. But there should not be such a situation.

There was no logical explanation for such a series of contradictions. Civilized men acted either this way or that. There could only be civilized men here, yet they acted neither this way nor that. Therefore—and the confusion began all over again.

Calhoun dictated an account of events to date into the emergency responder in the ship. If a search call came from space, the responder would broadcast this data and Calhoun's intended action. He carefully shut off all other operating circuits so the ship couldn't be found by their radiation. He equipped himself for travel, and he and Murgatroyd left the ship. Obviously, he headed toward the city where whatever was wrong was centered.

Travel on foot was unaccustomed, but not difficult. The vegetation was semi-familiar. Maris III was an Earth-type planet and circled a Sol-type sun, and given similar conditions of gravity, air, sunlight, and temperature range, similar organisms should develop. There would be room, for example, for low-growing ground-cover plants, and there would also be advantages to height. There would be some equivalent of grass, and there would be the equivalent of trees, with intermediate forms having in-between habits of growth. Similar reasoning would apply to animal life. There would be parallel ecological niches for animals to fill, and animals would adapt to fill them.

Maris III was not, then, an "unearthly" environment. It was much more like an unfamiliar part of a known planet than a new world altogether. But there were some oddities. An herbivorous creature without legs which squirmed like a snake. A pigeon-sized creature whose wings were modified, gossamer-thin scales with iridescent colorings. There were creatures which seemed to live in lunatic association, and Calhoun was irritably curious to know if they were really symbiotes or only unrecognizable forms of the same organism, like the terrestrial male and female firefly-glowworm.

But he was heading for the city. He couldn't spare time to biologize. On his first day's journey he looked for food to save the rations he carried. Murgatroyd was handy here. The little *tormal* had his place in human society. He was friendly, and he was passionately imitative of human beings, and he had a definite psychology of his own. But he was useful, too. When Calhoun strode through the forests, which had such curiously unleaflike foliage, Murgatroyd strode grandly with him, imitating his walk. From time to time he dropped to all four paws to investigate something. He invariably caught up with Calhoun within seconds.

Once Calhoun saw him interestedly bite a tiny bit out of a most unpromising-looking shrub stalk. He savored its flavor, and then swallowed it. Calhoun took note of the plant and cut off a section. He bound it to the skin of his arm up near the elbow. Hours later there was no allergic reaction, so he tasted it. It was almost familiar. It had the flavor of a bracken shoot, mingled with a fruity taste. It would be a green bulk-food like spinach or asparagus, filling but without much substance.

Later, Murgatroyd carefully examined a luscious-seeming fruit which grew low enough for him to pluck. He sniffed it closely and drew back. Calhoun noted that plant, too. Murgatroyd's tribe was bred at headquarters for some highly valuable qualities. One was a very sensitive stomach—but it was only one. Murgatroyd's metabolism was very close to man's. If he ate something and it didn't disagree with him, it was very likely safe for a man to eat it too. If he rejected something, it probably wasn't. But his real value was much more important than the tasting of questionable foods.

When Calhoun camped the first night, he made a fire of a plant shaped like a cactus barrel and permeated with oil. By heaping dirt around it, he confined its burning to a round space very much like the direct-heat element of an electronic stove. It was an odd illustration of the fact that human progress does not involve anything really new in kind, but only increased convenience and availability of highly primitive comforts. By the light of that circular bonfire, Calhoun actually read a little. But the light was inadequate. Presently he yawned. One did not get very far in the Med Service without knowing probability in human conduct. It enabled one to check on the accuracy of statements made, whether by patients or officials, to a Med Ship man. Today, though, he'd traveled a long way on foot. He glanced at Murgatroyd, who was gravely pretending to read from a singularly straight-edged leaf.

"Murgatroyd," said Calhoun, "it is likely that you will interpret any strange sound as a possible undersirable subjective experience. Which is to say, as dangerous. So if you hear anything sizable coming close during the night, I hope you'll squeal. Thank you."

Murgatroyd said *"Chee,"* and Calhoun rolled over and went to sleep.

It was mid-morning of the next day when he came upon a cultivated field. It had been cleared and planted, of course, in preparation for the colonists who'd been expected to occupy the city. Familiar Earth plants grew in it, ten feet high and more. And Calhoun examined it carefully, in the hope of finding how long since it had received attention. In his examination, he found the dead man.

As a corpse, the man was brand new, and Calhoun very carefully put himself into a strictly medical frame of mind before he bent over for a technical estimate of what had happened, and when. The dead man seemed to have died of hunger. He was terribly emaciated, and he didn't belong in a cultivated field far from the city. By his garments he was a city dweller and a prosperous one. He wore the jewels which nowadays indicated a man's profession and status in it much more than the value of his possessions. There was money in his pockets, and writing materials, a wallet with pictures and identification, and the normal oddments a man would carry. He'd been a civil servant of the city. And he shouldn't have died of starvation.

He especially shouldn't have gone hungry here! The sweet maize plants were tall and green. Their ears were ripe. He hadn't gone hungry! There were the inedible remains of at least two dozen sweet maize ears. They had been eaten some time—some days—ago, and one had been left unfinished. If the dead man had eaten them but was unable to digest them, his belly should have been swollen with undigested food. It wasn't. He'd eaten and digested and still had died, at least largely of inanition.

Calhoun scowled.

"How about this corn, Murgatroyd?" he demanded.

He reached up and broke off a half-yard-long ear. He stripped away the protecting, stringy leaves. The soft grains underneath looked appetizing. They smelled like good fresh food. Calhoun offered the ear to Murgatroyd.

The little *tormal* took it in his paws and on the instant was eating it with gusto.

"If you keep it down, he didn't die of eating it," said Calhoun, frowning. "And if he ate it—which he did—he didn't die of starvation. Which he did."

He waited. Murgatroyd consumed every grain upon the oversized cob. His furry belly distended a little. Calhoun offered him a second ear. He set to work on that, too, with self-evident enjoyment.

"In all history," said Calhoun, "nobody's ever been able to poison one of you *tormals* because of your digestive system has a qualitative analysis unit in it that yells bloody murder if anything's likely to disagree with you. As a probability of *tormal* reaction, you'd have been nauseated before now if that stuff wasn't good to eat."

But Murgatroyd ate until he was distinctly pot-bellied. He left a few grains on the second ear with obvious regret. He put it down carefully on the ground. He shifted his left-hand whiskers with his paw and elaborately licked them clean. He did the same to the whiskers on the right-hand side of his mouth. He said comfortably:

"*Chee!*"

"Then that's that," Calhoun told him. "This man didn't die of starvation. I'm getting queasy!"

He had his lab kit in his shoulder pack, of course. It was an absurdly small outfit, with almost microscopic instruments. But in Med Ship field work the techniques of microanalysis were standard. Distastefully, Calhoun took the tiny tissue sample from which he could gather necessary information. Standing, he ran through the analytic process that seemed called for. When he finished, he buried the dead man as well as he could and started off in the direction of the city again. He scowled as he walked.

He journeyed for nearly half an hour before he spoke. Murgatroyd accompanied him on all fours now because of his heavy meal. After a mile and a half, Calhoun stopped and said grimly:

"Let's check you over, Murgatroyd."

He verified the *tormal's* pulse and respiration and temperature. He put a tiny breath sample through the part of the lab kit which read off a basic metabolism rate. The small animal was quite accustomed to the process. He submitted blandly. The result of the checkover was that Murgatroyd the *tormal* was perfectly normal.

"But," said Calhoun angrily, "that man died of starvation! There was practically no fat in the tissue sample at all! He arrived where we found him while he was strong enough to eat, and he stayed where there was good food, and he ate it, and he digested it, and he died of starvation: Why?"

Murgatroyd wriggled unhappily, because Calhoun's tone was accusing. He said, "*Chee!*" in a subdued tone of voice. He looked pleadingly up at Calhoun.

"I'm not angry with you," Calhoun told him, "but dammit—"

He packed the lab kit back into his pack, which contained food for the two of them for about a week.

"Come along!" he said bitterly. He started off. Ten minutes

later he stopped. "What I said was impossible. But it happened, so it mustn't have been what I said. I must have
stated it wrongly. He could eat, because he did. He did eat,
because of the cobs left. He did digest it. So why did he
die of starvation? Did he stop eating?"

"*Chee!*" said Murgatroyd with conviction.

Calhoun grunted and marched on once more. The man had
not died of a disease, not directly. The tissue analysis gave
a picture of death which denied that it came of any organ
ceasing to function. Was it the failure of the organism—the
man—to take the action required for living? Had he stopped
eating?

Calhoun's mind skirted the notion warily. It was not
plausible. The man had been able to feed himself and had
done so. Anything which came upon him and made him unable to feed himself . . .

"He was a city man," growled Calhoun, "and this is a
damned long way from the city. What was he doing out
here, anyhow?"

He hesitated and tramped on again. A city man found
starved in a remote place might have become lost, somehow
or other. But if this man was lost, he was assuredly not
without food.

"He belonged in the city," said Calhoun vexedly, "and
he left it. The city's almost but not quite empty. Our would-
be murderers are in it. This is a new colony. There was a
city to be built and fields to be plowed and planted, and
then a population was to come here from Dettra Two. The
city's built and the fields are plowed and planted. Where's
the population?"

He scowled thoughtfully at the ground before him. Murgatroyd tried to scowl too, but he wasn't very successful.

"What's the answer, Murgatroyd? Did the man come away
from the city because he had a disease? Was he driven out?"

"*Chee*," said Murgatroyd without conviction.

"I don't know either," admitted Calhoun. "He walked out
into the middle of that field and then stopped walking. He
was hungry and he ate. He digested. He stayed there for
days. Why? Was he waiting to die of something? Presently

he stopped eating. He died. What made him leave the city? What made him stop eating? Why did he die?"

Murgatroyd investigated a small plant and decided that it was not interesting. He came back to Calhoun.

"He wasn't killed," said Calhoun, "but somebody tried to kill us—somebody who's in the city now. That man could have come out here to keep from being killed by the same people. Yet he died anyhow. Why'd they want to kill him? Why'd they want to kill us? Because we were a Med Ship? Because they didn't want Med Service to know there was a disease here? Ridiculous!"

"Chee," said Murgatroyd.

"I don't like the looks of things," said Calhoun. "For instance, in any ecological system there are always carrion eaters. At least some of them fly. There would be plain signs if the city was full of corpses. There aren't any. On the other hand, if the city was inhabited, and there was sickness, they would welcome a Med Ship with open arms. But that dead man didn't come away from the city in any ordinary course of events, and he didn't die in any conventional fashion. There's an empty city and an improbable dead man and a still more improbable attempt at murder! What gives, Murgatroyd?"

Murgatroyd took hold of Calhoun's hand and tugged at it. He was bored. Calhoun moved on slowly.

"Paradoxes don't turn up in nature," said Calhoun darkly. "Things that happen naturally never contradict each other. You only get such things when men try to do things that don't fit together—like having a plague and trying to destroy a Med Ship, if that's the case, and living in a city and not showing on its streets, if that is occurring, and dying of starvation while one's digestion is good and there's food within hand's reach. And that did happen! There was dirty work at the spaceport, Murgatroyd. I suspect dirty work at every crossroad. Keep your eyes open."

"Chee," said Murgatroyd. Calhoun was fully in motion, now, and Murgatroyd let go of his hand and went on ahead to look things over.

Calhoun crossed the top of a rounded hillcrest some three

miles from the shallow grave he'd made. He began to accept the idea that the dead man had stopped eating for some reason, as the only possible explanation of his death. But that didn't make it plausible. He saw another ridge of hills ahead.

In another hour he came to the crest of that farther range. It was the worn-down remnant of a very ancient mountain chain, now eroded to a mere fifteen hundred or two thousand feet. He stopped at the very top. Here was a time and place to look and take note of what he saw. The ground stretched away in gently rolling fashion for very many miles, and there was the blue blink of sea at the horizon. A little to the left he saw shining white. He grunted.

That was the city of Maris III, which had been built to receive colonists from Dettra and relieve the population pressure there. It had been planned as the nucleus of a splendid, spacious, civilized world-nation to be added to the number of human-occupied worlds. From its beginning it should have held a population in the hundreds of thousands. It was surrounded by cultivated fields, and the air above it should have been a-shimmer with flying things belonging to its inhabitants.

Calhoun stared at it through his binoculars. They could not make an image, even so near, to compare with that which the electron telescope had made from space, but he could see much. The city was perfect. It was intact. It was new. But there was no sign of occupancy anywhere. It did not look dead, so much as frozen. There were no fliers above it. There was no motion on the highways. He saw one straight road which ran directly away along his line of sight. Had there been vehicles on it, he would have seen at least shifting patches of color as clots of traffic moved together. There were none.

He pressed his lips together and began to inspect the nearer terrain. He saw foreshortened areas where square miles of ground had been cleared and planted with Earth vegetation. This was a complicated process. First the ground had to be bulldozed clean, and then great sterilizers had to lumber back and forth, killing every native seed and root and even the native soil bacteria. Then the land had to be sprayed with cultures of the nitrogen-fixing and phosphorous-releasing microscopic organisms which normally live in symbiosis with Earth plants. These had to be tested beforehand for their ability to compete with indigenous bacterial life. And then Earth plants could be sown.

They had been. Calhoun saw that inimitable green which a man somehow always recognizes. It is the green of plants whose ancestors throve on Earth and which have followed that old planet's children halfway across the galaxy.

"There's a look to a well-tended field," said Calhoun, after a long look through binoculars, "that shows what kind of people cultivated it. There are fields up ahead that are well laid out, but nobody's touched them for weeks. The furrows are straight and the crops healthy. But they're beginning to show neglect. If the city was finished and waiting for its population, there would be caretakers tending the fields until the people came. There's been no caretaking done here!"

Murgatroyd stared wisely about as he considered Calhoun to be doing.

"In short," said Calhoun, "something's happened that I don't like. The population must be nearly zero or the fields would have been kept right. One man can keep a hell of a lot of ground in good shape, with modern machinery. People don't plant fields with the intention to neglect them. There's been a considerable change of plans around here. Enmity to a Med Ship is something more than a random impulse." Calhoun was not pleased. With the vision screens of his ship burned out, a return to headquarters was out of the question. "Whoever was handling the landing grid doesn't want help. He doesn't even want visitors. But Med Service was notified to come and look over the new colony. Either somebody changed his views drastically, or the people in charge of the landing grid aren't the ones who asked for a public health checkup."

Murgatroyd said profoundly:

"*Chee!*"

"The poor devil I buried even seems to hint at something of the sort. He could have used help! Maybe there are two kinds of people here. One kind doesn't want aid and tried to kill us because we'd offer it. The other kind needs it. If so, there might be a certain antagonism . . ."

He stared with knitted brows over the vast expanse toward the horizon. Murgatroyd, at this moment, was a little way behind Calhoun. He stood up on his hind legs and stared intently off to one side. He shaded his eyes with a forepaw in a singularly humanlike fashion and looked inquisitively at something he saw. Calhoun did not notice.

"Make a guess, Murgatroyd," he commanded. "Make a wild one. A dead man who'd no reason for dying. Live people who should have no reason for wanting to spatter us against the walls of our Med Ship. Something was fatal to that dead man. Somebody tried to be fatal to us. Is there a connection?"

Murgatroyd stared absorbedly at a patch of brushwood some fifty yards to his left. Calhoun started down the hillside. Murgatroyd remained fixed in a pose of intensely curious attention to the patch of brush. Calhoun went on. His back was toward the brush thicket.

There was a deep-toned, musical twanging sound from the thicket. Calhoun's body jerked violently from an impact. He stumbled and went down, with the shaft of a wooden projectile sticking out of his back. He lay still.

Murgatroyd whimpered. He rushed to where Calhoun lay upon the ground. He danced in agitation, chattering shrilly. He wrung his paws in humanlike distress. He tugged at Calhoun, but Calhoun made no response.

A girl emerged from the thicket. She was gaunt and thin, yet her garments had once been of admirable quality. She carried a strange and utterly primitive weapon. She moved toward Calhoun, bent over him and laid a hand to the wooden projectile she had fired into his back.

He moved suddenly. He grappled. The girl toppled, and he swarmed upon her savagely as she struggled. But she was taken by surprise. There was the sound of panting, and Murgatroyd danced in a fever of anxiety.

Then Calhoun stood up quickly. He stared down at the emaciated girl who had tried to murder him from ambush.

She was panting horribly now.

"Really," said Calhoun in a professional tone, "as a doctor I'd say that you should be in bed instead of wandering around trying to murder total strangers. When did this trouble begin? I'm going to take your temperature and your pulse. Murgatroyd and I have been hoping to find someone like you. The only other human being I've met on this planet wasn't able to talk."

He swung his shoulder pack around and impatiently jerked a sharp-pointed stick out of it. It was the missile, which had been stopped by the pack. He brought out his lab kit. With absolute absorption in the task, he prepared to make a swift check of his would-be murderer's state of health.

It was not good. There was already marked emaciation. The desperately panting girl's eyes were deep-sunk, hollow. She gasped and gasped. Still gasping, she lapsed into unconsciousness.

"Here," said Calhoun curtly, "you enter the picture, Murgatroyd. This is the sort of thing you're designed to handle."

He set to work briskly. Presently he observed:

"Besides a delicate digestion and a hair-trigger antibody system, Murgatroyd, you ought to have the instincts of a watchdog. I don't like coming that close to being shot by a lady patient. See if there's anybody else around, will you?"

"Chee" said Murgatroyd shrilly. But he didn't understand. He watched as Calhoun deftly drew a small sample of blood from the unconscious girl's arm and painstakingly put half the tiny quantity into an almost microscopic ampoule in the Lab kit. Then he moved toward Murgatroyd.

The tormal wriggled as Calhoun made the injection. But it did not hurt. There was an insensitive spot on his flank where the nerves had been blocked off before he was a week old.

"As one medical man to another," said Calhoun, "you've noticed that the symptoms are of anoxia—oxygen starvation. Which doesn't make sense in the open air where we're breathing comfortably. Another paradox, Murgatroyd! But there's an emergency, too. How can you relieve anoxia when you haven't any oxygen?"

He looked down at the unconscious girl. She displayed the same sort of emaciation he'd noted in the dead man in the field some miles back. Patients with a given disease often acquire a certain odd resemblance to each other. This girl seemed to be in an earlier stage of whatever had killed the civil servant in the corn field. He'd died of starvation with partly eaten food by his hand. She'd tried to murder Calhoun, just as persons unknown, in the city, had tried to kill both Calhoun and Murgatroyd in the Med Ship some forty thousand miles out in space. But her equipment for murder was not on a par with that of the operators of the landing grid. She didn't belong in their class. She might be a fugitive from them.

Calhoun put these things together. Then he swore in sudden, bitter anger. He stopped abruptly, in concern lest she'd heard.

She hadn't. She was still insensible.

CHAPTER III

"That pattern of human conduct which is loosely called 'self-respecting' has the curious property of restricting to the individual, through his withdrawal of acts to communicate misfortune, the unfavorable chance occurrences which probability insists must take place. On the other hand, the same pattern of human conduct tends to disseminate and to share chance favorable occurrences among the group. The members of a group of persons practising 'self-respect,' then, increase the mathematical probability of good fortune to all their number. This explains the instability of cultures in which principles leading to this type of behavior become obsolete. A decadent society brings bad luck upon itself by the operation of the laws of probability . . ."

Probability and Human Conduct——Fitzgerald

SHE CAME very slowly back to consciousness. It was almost as if she waked from utterly exhausted sleep. When she first opened her eyes, they wandered vaguely until they fell upon Calhoun. Then a bitter and contemptuous hatred filled them. Her hand fumbled weakly to the knife at her waist. It was not a good weapon. It had been table cutlery, and the handle was much too slender to permit a grip by which somebody could be killed. Calhoun bent over and took the knife away from her. It had been ground unskillfully to a point.

"In my capacity as your doctor," he told her, "I must forbid you to stab me. It wouldn't be good for you." Then he said, "Look, my name's Calhoun. I came from Sector Med Headquarters to make a planetary health inspection here, and some lads in the city apparently didn't want a Med Ship aground. So they tried to kill me by buttering me all over the walls of my ship with the landing-grid field. I made what was practically a crash landing, and now I need to know what's up."

The burning hatred remained in her eyes, but there was a trace of doubt.

"Here," said Calhoun, "is my identification."

He showed her the highly official documents which gave him vast authority—where a planetary government was willing to concede it.

"Of course," he added, "papers can be stolen. But I have a witness that I'm what and who I say I am. You've heard of tormals? Murgatroyd will vouch for me."

He called his small and furry companion. Murgatroyd advanced and politely offered a small, prehensile paw. He said "Chee" in his shrill voice, and then solemnly took hold of the girl's wrist in imitation of Calhoun's previous action of feeling her pulse.

Calhoun watched. The girl stared at Murgatroyd. But all the galaxy had heard of tormals. They'd been found on a planet in the Deneb region, and they were engaging pets and displayed an extraordinary immunity to the diseases men were apt to scatter in their interstellar journeying. A forgotten Med Service researcher made an investigation of the ability of tormals to live in contact with men. He came up with a discovery which made them very much too valuable to have their lives wasted in mere sociability. There were

still not enough of Murgatroyd's kind to meet the need that
men had of them, and laymen had to forego their distinctly
charming society. So Murgatroyd was an identification.

The girl said faintly:

"If you'd only come earlier . . . but it's too late now. I—I
thought you came from the city."

"I was headed there," said Calhoun.

"They'll kill you."

"Yes," agreed Calhoun, "they probably will. But right now
you're ill and I'm Med Service. I suspect there's been an
epidemic of some disease here, and that for some reason
the people in the city don't want the Med Service to know
about it. You seem to have it, whatever it is. Also, that was
a very curious weapon you shot me with."

The girl said drearily:

"One of our group had made a hobby of such things.
Ancient weapons. He had bows and arrows and—what I
shot you with was a crossbow. It doesn't need power. Not
even chemical explosives. So when we ran away from the city,
he ventured back in and armed us as well as he could."

Calhoun nodded. A little irrelevant talk is always useful
at the beginning of a patient-interviewer. But what she said
was not irrelevant. A group of people had fled the city.
They'd needed arms, and one of their number had gone back
into the city for them. He'd known where to find reconstruc-
tions of ancient lethal devices—a hobby collection. It sounded
like people of the civil service type. Of course there were
no longer social classes separated by income. Not on most
worlds, anyhow. But there were social groupings based on
similar tastes, which had led to similar occupations and went
on to natural congeniality. Calhoun placed her now. He
remembered a long-outmoded term, "upper middle class,"
which no longer meant anything in economics but did in
medicine.

"I'd like a case history," he said conversationally. "Name?"

"Helen Jons," she said wearily.

He held the mike of his pocket recorder to pick up her
answers. Occupation: statistician. She'd been a member of
the office force which was needed during the building of the

city. When the construction work was finished, most of the workmen returned to the mother-world Dettra, but the office staff stayed on to organize things when the colonists arrived.

"Hold it," said Calhoun. "You were a member of the office staff who stayed in the city to wait for the colonists. But a moment ago you said you fled from the city. There are still some people there, at least around the landing grid. I've reason to be sure of it. Were they part of the office staff too? If not, where did they come from?"

She shook her head weakly.

"Who are they?" he repeated.

"I don't know," she said drearily. "They came after the plague."

"Oh," said Calhoun. "Go on. When did the plague turn up? And how?"

She continued in a feeble voice. The plague appeared among the last shipload of workmen waiting to be returned to the mother world. There were then about a thousand people in the city, of all classes and occupations. The disease appeared first among those who tended the vast fields of planted crops.

It was well established before its existence was suspected. There were no obvious early symptoms, but those affected felt a loss of energy and they became listless and lacadaisical. The listlessness showed first in a cessation of griping and quarreling among the workmen. Normal, healthy human beings are aggressive. They squabble with each other as a matter of course. But squabbling ceased. Men hadn't the energy for it.

Shortness of breath appeared later. It wasn't obvious, at first. Men who lacked energy to squabble wouldn't exert themselves and so get out of breath. It was one of the medical staff who drove himself impatiently in spite of what he thought was a transient weariness, and discovered himself gasping without cause. He took a metabolism test, suspicious because the symptoms were so extreme. His metabolic rate was astonishingly low.

"Hold it again," commanded Calhoun. "You're a statistician, but you're talking medical talk. How's that?"

"Kim," said the girl tiredly. "He was on the medical staff.

I was—I was going to marry him."

Calhoun nodded.

"Go on."

She seemed to need to gather strength even to talk. She did not go on. Shortness of breath among the plague victims was progressive. Presently they gasped horribly from the exertion of getting to their feet, even. Walking, however slowly, could be done only at the cost of panting for breath. After a certain time they simply lay still. They could not summon the energy to stir. Then they sank into unconsciousness and died.

"What did the doctors think about all this?" demanded Calhoun.

"Kim could tell you," said the girl exhaustedly. "The doctors worked frantically. They tried everything—everything! They could get the symptoms in experimental animals, but they couldn't isolate the germ or whatever it was that caused the disease. Kim said they couldn't get a pure culture. It was incredible. No technique would isolate the cause of the symptoms, and yet the plague was contagious. Terribly so!"

Calhoun scowled. A new pathogenic mechanism was always possible, but it was at least unlikely. Still, something that standard bacteriological methods couldn't track down was definitely a job for the Med Service. But there were people in the city who didn't want the Med Service to interfere. The girl hadn't referred to them once, when she spoke of a flight from the city, and again when she said someone ventured back for weapons. And she'd used a weapon on him, thinking him from the city. The description of the plague, too, was remarkable.

It was able to hide from men, which was something no other microorganism could accomplish. It was an ability that would offer no advantage to a disease germ in a state of purely natural happenings. Disease germs do not encounter bacteriological laboratories, as a rule, often enough to need to adapt to escape them. It would not help an average germ or microbe to be invisible to an electron microscope. There would be no reason for such invisibility to be developed.

But more than that, why should anybody want to keep a

Med Service man like Calhoun from investigating a plague?
When infected people fled from the city to die in the wilds,
why should people remaining in the city try to destroy a
Med Ship which might help to end the deaths? Ordinarily,
well people in the middle of an epidemic are terrified lest
they catch it. They'd be as anxious for Med Service help as
those already infected. What was going on here?

"You said about a thousand people were in the city,"
observed Calhoun. "They tended the crops and waited for
the city's permanent inhabitants. What happened after the
plague was recognized to be one?"

"The first shipload of emigrants came from Dettra Two,"
said the girl hopelessly. "We didn't bring them to ground with
the landing grid. Instead, we described the plague. We
warned them away. We quarantined ourselves while our
doctors tried to fight the disease. The shipload of new people
went back to Dettra without landing."

Calhoun nodded. This would be normal.

"Then another ship came. There were maybe two hundred
of us left alive. More than half of us already showed signs of
the plague. This other ship came. It landed on emergency
rockets because we had nobody left who knew how to work
the grid."

Then her voice wavered a little as she told of the landing
of the strange ship in the landing grid of the city that was
dying without ever having really lived. There was no crowd
to meet the ship. Those people who were not yet stricken
had abandoned the city and scattered themselves widely,
hoping to escape contagion by isolating themselves in new
and uncontaminated dwelling units. But there was no lack of
communication facilities. Nearly all the survivors watched
the ship come down through vision screens in the control
building of the then-useless grid.

The ship touched ground. Men came out. They did not
look like doctors. They did not act like them. The vision
screens, in the control building were snapped off immediately.
Contact could not be restored. So the isolated groups spoke
agitatedly to each other by vision screen. They exchanged
messages of desperate hope. Then, newly landed men ap-

peared at an apartment whose occupant was in the act of such a conversation with a group in a distant building. He left the visiphone on as he went to admit and greet the men he hoped were researchers, at least, come to find the cause of the plague and end it.

The viewers at the other visiphone plate gazed eagerly into his apartment. They saw the group of newcomers enter. They saw them deliberately murder their friend and the survivors of his family.

Plague-stricken or merely terrified people—in pairs or trios widely separated through the city—communicated in swift desperation. It was possible that there had been a mistake, a blunder, and an unauthorized crime had been committed. But it was not a mistake. Unthinkable as such an idea was, there developed proof that the plague on Maris III was to be ended as if it were an epizootic among animals. Those who had it and those who had been exposed to it were to be killed to prevent its spread among the newcomers.

A conviction of such horror could not be accepted without absolute proof. But when night fell, the public power supply of the city was cut off and communications ended. The singular sunset hush of Maris III left utter stillness everywhere—except for the screams which echoed among the city's innumerable empty-eyed, unoccupied buildings.

The scant remainder of the plague survivors fled in the night. They fled singly and in groups, carrying the plague with them. Some carried members of their families who were too weak to walk. Others helped already-doomed wives or friends or husbands to the open country. Flight would not save their lives. It would only prevent their murder. But somehow that seemed a thing to be attempted.

"This," said Calhoun, "is not a history of your own case. When did you develop the disease, whatever it may be?"

"Don't you know what it is?" asked Helen hopelessly.

"Not yet," admitted Calhoun. "I've very little information. I'm trying to get more."

He did not mention the information gathered from a dead man in a corn field some miles away.

The girl told of her own case. The first symptom was listlessness. She could pull out of it by making an effort, but it progressed. Day by day more urgent, more violent effort was needed to pay attention to anything, and she noted greater weakness when she tried to act. She felt no discomfort, not even hunger or thirst. She'd had to summon increasing resolution even to become aware of the need to do anything at all.

The symptoms were singularly like those of a man too long at too high an altitude without oxygen. They were even more like those of a man in a non-pressurized flier, whose oxygen supply was cut off. Such a man would pass out without realizing that he was slipping into unconsciousness, only it would happen in minutes. Here the process was infinitely gradual. It was a matter of weeks. But it was the same thing.

"I'd been infected before we ran away," said Helen drearily. "I didn't know it then. Now I know I've a few more days of being able to think and act, if I try hard enough. But it'll be less and less each day. Then I'll stop being able to try."

Calhoun watched the tiny recorder roll its multiple-channel tape from one spool to the other as she talked.

"You had energy enough to try to kill me," he observed.

He looked at the weapon. There was an arched steel spring placed crosswise at the end of a barrel like a sporting blast-gun. Now he saw a handle and a ratchet by which the spring was brought to tension, storing up power to throw the missile. He asked:

"Who wound up this crossbow?"

Helen hesitated. "Kim—Kim Walpole," she said finally.

"You're not a solitary refugee now? There are others of your group still alive?"

She hesitated again, and then said:

"Some of us came to realize that staying apart didn't matter. We couldn't hope to live anyhow. We already had the plague. Kim is one of us. He's the strongest. He wound up the crossbow for me. He had the weapons to begin with."

Calhoun asked seemingly casual questions. She told him of a group of fugitives remaining together because all were already doomed. There had been eleven of them. Two were

dead now. Three others were in the last lethargy. It was
impossible to feed them. They were dying. The strongest was
Kim Walpole, who'd ventured back into the city to bring
out weapons for the rest. He'd led them, and now was still
the strongest and—so the girl considered—the wisest of them
all.

They were waiting to die. But the newcomers to the planet
—the invaders, they believed—were not content to let them
wait. Groups of hunters came out of the city and searched
for them.

"Probably," said the girl dispassionately, "to burn our
bodies against contagion. They kill us so they won't have to
wait. And it just seemed so horrible that we felt we ought
to defend our right to die naturally. That's why I shot at you.
I shouldn't have, but . . ."

She stopped helplessly. Calhoun nodded.

The fugitives now aided each other simply to avoid
murder. They gathered together exhaustedly at nightfall, and
those who were strongest did what they could for the others.
By day, those who could walk scattered to separate hiding
places, so that if one was discovered, the others might still
escape the indignity of being butchered. They had no stronger
motive than that. They were merely trying to die with dignity,
instead of being killed as sick beasts. Which bespoke a tradition and an attitude that Calhoun approved. People like
these would know something of the science of probability in
human conduct. Only they would call it ethics. But the
strangers—the invaders—were of another type. They probably
came from another world.

"I don't like this," said Calhoun coldly. "Just a moment."

He went over to Murgatroyd. Murgatroyd seemed to
droop a little. Calhoun checked his breathing and listened
to his heart. Murgatroyd submitted, saying only "*Chee*" when
Calhoun put him down.

"I'm going to help you to your rendevous," said Calhoun
abruptly. "Murgatroyd's got the plague now. I exposed him
to it, and he's reacting fast. And I want to see the others
of your group before nightfall."

The girl just managed to get to her feet. Even speaking

had tired her, but she gamely though wearily moved off at a slant to the hillside's slope. Calhoun picked up the odd weapon and examined it thoughtfully. He wound it up as it was obviously meant to be. He picked up the missile it had fired, and put it in place. He went after the girl, carrying it. Murgatroyd brought up the rear.

Within a quarter of a mile the girl stopped and clung swaying to the trunk of a slender tree. It was plain that she had to rest, and dreaded getting off her feet because of the desperate effort needed to arise.

"I'm going to carry you," said Calhoun firmly. "You tell me the way."

He picked her up bodily and marched on. She was light. She was not a large girl, but she should have weighed more. Calhoun still carried the quaint antique weapon without difficulty.

Murgatroyd followed as Calhoun went up a small incline on the greater hillside and down a very narrow ravine. Through brushwood he pushed until he came to a small open space where shelters had been made for a dozen or so human beings. They were utterly primitive—merely roofs of leafy branches over framework of sticks. But of course they were not intended for permanent use. They were meant only to protect plague-stricken folk while they waited to die.

But there was disaster here. Calhoun saw it before the girl could. There were beds of leaves underneath the shelters. There were three bodies lying upon them. They would be those refugees in the terminal coma which, since the girl had described it, accounted for the dead man Calhoun had found, dead of starvation with food plants all around him. But now Calhoun saw something more. He swung the girl swiftly in his arms so that she would not see. He put her gently down and said:

"Stay still. Don't move. Don't turn."

He went to make sure. A moment later he raged. It was Calhoun's profession to combat death and illness in all its forms, and he took his profession seriously. There are defeats, of course, which a medical man has to accept, though unwillingly. But nobody in the profession, and least of all a

Med Ship man, could fail to be roused to fury by the sight of people who should have been his patients, lying utterly still with their throats cut.

He covered them with branches. He went back to Helen.

"This place has been found by somebody from the city," he told her harshly. "The men in coma have been murdered. I advise you not to look. At a guess, whoever did it is now trying to track down the rest of you."

He went grimly over the small open glade, searching the ground for footprints. There was ground-cover at most places, but at the edge of the clearing he found one set of heavy footprints leading away. He put his own foot beside a print and rested his weight on it. His foot made a lesser depression. The other print had been made by a man weighing more than Calhoun. Therefore it was not one of the party of plague victims.

He found another set of such footprints, entering the glade from another spot.

"One man only," he said icily. "He won't think he has to be on guard, because a city's administrative personnel—such as was left behind for the plague to hit—doesn't usually have weapons among their possessions. And he's confident that all of you are weak enough not to be dangerous to him."

Helen did not turn pale. She was pale before. She stared numbly at Calhoun. He looked grimly at the sky.

"It'll be sunset within the hour," he said savagely. "If it's the intention of the newcomers—the invaders—to burn the bodies of all plague victims, he'll come back here to dispose of these three. He didn't do it before lest the smoke warn the rest of you. But he knows the shelters held more than three people. He'll be back!"

Murgatroyd said "Chee!" in a bewildered fashion. He was on all fours, and he regarded his paws as if they did not belong to him. He panted.

Calhoun checked him over. Respiration away up. Heart action like that of the girl Helen. His temperature was not up, but down. Calhoun said remorsefully:

"You and I, Murgatroyd, have a bad time of it in our profession. But mine is the worse. You don't have to play dirty tricks on me, and I've had to, on you!"

Murgatroyd said "*Chee!*" and whimpered. Calhoun laid him gently on a bed of leaves which was not occupied by a murdered man.

"Lie still!" he commanded. "Exercise is bad for you."

He walked away. Murgatroyd whined faintly, but lay still as if exhausted.

"I'm going to move you," Calhoun told the girl, "so you won't be sighted if that man from the city comes back. And I've got to keep out of sight for a while or your friends will mistake me for him. I count on you to vouch for me later. Basically, I'm making an ambush." Then he explained irritably, "I daren't try to trail him because he might not backtrack to return here."

He lifted the girl and placed her where she could see the glade in its entirety, but would not be visible. He settled down himself a little distance away. He was acutely dissatisfied with the measures he was forced to take. He could not follow the murderer and leave Helen and Murgatroyd unprotected, even though the murderer might find another victim because he was not being trailed. In any case Murgatroyd's life, just now, was more important than the life of any human being on Maris III. On him depended everything.

But Calhoun was not pleased with himself at all.

There was silence except for the normal noises of living wild things. There were fluting sounds, which later Calhoun would be told came from crawling creatures not too much unlike the land turtles of Earth. There were deep-bass hummings, which came from the throats of miniature creatures which might roughly be described as birds. There were chirpings which were the cries of what might be approximately described as wild pigs, except that they weren't. But the sun Maris sank low toward the nearer hillcrests, and behind them, and there came a strange, expectant hush over all the landscape. At sundown on Maris III there is a singular period when the creatures of the day are silent and those of the night are not yet active. Nothing moved. Nothing stirred. Even the improbable foliage was still.

It was into this stillness and this half-light that small and intermittent rustling sounds entered. Presently there was a faint murmur of speech. A tall, gaunt young man came out of the brushwood, supporting a pathetically feeble old man, barely able to walk. Calhoun made a gesture of warning as the girl Helen opened her lips to speak. The slowly moving pair came into the glade, the young man moving exhaustedly, the older man staggering with weakness despite his help. The younger helped the older to sit down. He stood panting.

A woman and a man came together, assisting each other. There was barely light enough from the sun's afterglow to show their faces, emaciated and white.

A fifth feeble figure came tottering out of another opening in the brush. He was dark-bearded and broad, and he had been a powerful man. But now the plague lay heavily upon him.

They greeted each other listlessly. They had not yet discovered those of their number who had been murdered.

The gaunt young man summoned his strength and moved toward the shelter where Calhoun had covered an unseemly sight with branches.

Murgatroyd whimpered.

There came another rustling sound, but this had nothing of feebleness in it. Branches were pushed forthrightly out of the way and a man came striding confidently into the small open space. He was well-fleshed, and his color was excellent. Calhoun automatically judged him to be in superlative good health, slightly overweight, and of that physical type which suffers very few psychosomatic troubles because it lives strictly and enjoyably in the present.

Calhoun stood up. He stepped out into the fading light just as the sturdy stranger grinned at the group of plague-stricken semi-skeletons.

"Back, eh?" he said amiably. "Saved me a lot of trouble. I'll make one job of it."

With leisurely confidence he reached to the blaster at his hip.

"Drop it!" snapped Calhoun from behind him. "Drop it!"

The sturdy man whirled. He saw Calhoun with a crossbow raised to cover him. There was light enough to show
that it was not a blast-rifle—in fact, that it was no weapon of
any kind modern men would ordinarily use. But much more
significant to the sturdy man was the fact that Calhoun wore
a uniform and was in good health.

He snatched out his blast-pistol with professional alertness.

And Calhoun shot him with the crossbow. It happened
that he shot him dead.

CHAPTER IV

"Statistically, it must be recognized that no human action is
without consequences to the man who acts. Again statistically, it
must be recognized that the consequences of an action tend with
strong probability to follow the general pattern of the action. A
violent action, for example, has a strong probability of violent
consequences, and since at least some of the consequences of an
act must affect the person acting, a man who acts violently exposes
himself to the probability that chance consequences which affect
him, if unfavorable, will be violently so."

Probability and Human Conduct——Fitzgerald

MURGATROYD had been inoculated with a blood sample from
the girl Helen some three hours or less before sunset. But
it was one of the more valuable genetic qualities of the
tormal race that they reacted to bacterial infection as a
human being reacts to medication. Medicine on the skin
of a human being rarely has any systemic effect. Medication
on mucous membrane penetrates better. Ingested medication
—medicine that is swallowed—has greater effectiveness still.
But substances injected into tissues or the bloodstream have
the most of all. A centigram of almost any drug administered
by injection will have an effect close to that of a gram taken
orally. It acts at once and here is no modification by gastric
juices.

Murgatroyd had had half a cubic centimeter of the girl's

blood injected into the spot on his flank where he could feel no pain. It contained the unknown cause of the plague on Maris III. Its effect as injected was incomparably greater than the same infective material smeared on his skin or swallowed. In either such case, of course, it would have had no effect at all, because *tormals* were to all intents and purposes immune to ordinary contagions. Just as they had a built-in unit in their digestive tract to cause the instant rejection of unwholesome food, their body cells had a built-in ability to produce antibodies immediately if the toxin of a pathogenic organism came into contact with them. So *tormals* were effectively safe against any disease transmitted by ordinary methods of infection. Yet if a culture of pathogenic bacteria, say, were injected into their bloodstream, their whole body set to work to turn out antibodies because their whole body was attacked, and all at once. There was practically no in-cubation-period.

Murgatroyd, who had been given the plague in mid-afternoon, was reacting violently to its toxins by sunset. But two hours after darkness fell he arose and said shrilly, "*Chee-chee-chee!*" He'd been sunk in heavy slumber. When he woke, there was a small fire in the glade, about which the exhausted, emaciated fugitives consulted with Calhoun. Calhoun was saying bitterly:

"The whole thing is wrong! It's self-contradictory, and that means a man, or men, trying to meddle with the way the universe was made to run. Those characters in the city aren't fighting the plague—they're co-operating with it! When I came in a Med Ship, they should have welcomed my help. Instead they tried to kill me so I couldn't perform the function I was made for and trained for! They're going against the way the universe works. From what Helen tells me, they landed with the purpose of helping the plague wipe out everybody else on the planet. They began their butchery immediately. That's why you people ran away."

The weary, weakened people listened almost numbly.

"The invaders—and that's what they are," said Calhoun angrily, "have to be immune and know it, or else they wouldn't risk contagion by tracking you down to murder you.

The city's infected and they're not alarmed. You're dying and they only try to hasten your death. I arrive, and I might be of use, so they try to kill me. They must know what the plague is and what it does, because their only criticism of it seems to be that it doesn't kill fast enough. And that is out of the ordinary course of nature. It's not intelligent human conduct."

Murgatroyd peered about. He'd just waked, and the look of his surroundings had changed entirely while he slept.

"A plague's not pleasant, but it's natural. This plague is neither pleasant *nor* natural. There's human interference with the normal course of events—certainly the way things are going is abnormal. I'm not too sure somebody didn't direct this from the beginning. That's why I shot that man with the crossbow instead of taking a blaster to him. I meant to wound him so I could make him answer questions, but the cross-bow's not an accurate weapon and it happened that I killed him instead. There wasn't much information in the stuff in his pockets. The only significant item was a ground-car key, and that only means there's a car waiting for him to come back from hunting you."

The gaunt young man said drearily:

"He didn't come from Dettra, which is our planet. Fashions are different on different worlds and he wears a uniform we don't have. His clothing uses fasteners we don't use, too. He's from another solar system entirely."

Murgatroyd saw Calhoun and rushed to him. He embraced Calhoun's legs with enthusiasm. He chattered shrilly of his relief at finding the man he knew. The skeletonlike plague victims stared at him.

"This," said Calhoun with infinite relief, "is Murgatroyd. He's had the plague and is over it. So now we'll get you people cured. I wish I had better light!"

He counted Murgatroyd's breathing and listened to his heart. Murgatroyd was in that state of boisterous good health which is standard in any well-cared-for lower animal, but amounts to genius in a *tormal*. Calhoun regarded him with deep satisfaction.

"All right!" he said. "Come along!"

He plucked a brand of burning resinous stuff from the campfire. He handed it to the gaunt young man and led the way. Murgatroyd ambled complacently after him. Calhoun stopped under one of the unoccupied shelters and got out his lab kit. He bent over Murgatroyd. What he did, did not hurt. When he stood up, he squinted at the red fluid in the instrument he'd used.

"About twenty cc's," he observed. "This is strictly emergency stuff I'm doing now. But I'd say that there's an emergency."

The gaunt young man said:

"I'd say you've doomed yourself. The incubation period seems to be about six days. It took that long to develop among the doctors we had on the office staff."

Calhoun opened a compartment of the kit, whose minuscule test tubes and pipettes gleamed in the torchlight. He absorbedly transferred the reddish fluid to a miniature filter-barrel, piercing a self-healing plastic cover to do so. He said:

"You're pre-med of course. The way you talk—"

"I was an interne," said Kim. "Now I'm pre-corpse."

"I doubt that last," said Calhoun. "But I wish I had some distilled water . . . this is anticoagulant." He added the trace of a drop to the sealed, ruddy fluid. He shook the whole filter to agitate it. The instrument was hardly larger than his thumb. "Now a clumper . . ." He added a minute quantity of a second substance from an almost microscopic ampule. He shook the filter again. "You can guess what I'm doing. With a decent lab I'd get the structure and formula of the antibody Murgatroyd has so obligingly turned out for us. We'd set to work synthesizing it, and in twenty hours we would have it coming out of the reaction flasks in quantity. But there is no lab."

"There's one in the city," said the gaunt young man hopelessly. "It was for the colonists who were to come. And we were staffed to give them proper medical care. When the plague came, our doctors did everything imaginable. They not only tried the usual culture tricks, but they cultured samples of every separate tissue in fatal cases. They never found a single organism, even with electron microscopes, that would produce the plague." He said with a sort of weary pride, "Those who'd been exposed worked until they had the plague, and then others took over. Every man worked as long as he could make his brain serve him."

Calhoun squinted through the glass tube of the filter at the light of the sputtering torch.

"Almost clumped," he said. Then he added, "I suspect there's been some very fine laboratory work done somewhere to give the invaders their confidence of immunity to this plague. They landed and instantly set to work to mop up the city—to complete the job the plague hadn't quite finished. I suspect there could have been some fine lab work done to make plague mechanism undetectable. I don't like the things I'm forced to suspect!"

He inspected the glass filter tube again.

"Somebody," he said coldly, "considered that my arrival would be an unfavorable circumstance to him and what he wanted to happen. I think it is. He tried to kill me. He didn't. I'm afraid I consider his existence an unfavorable circumstance." He paused, and said very measuredly, "Co-operating with a plague is a highly technical business; it needs as much information as fighting a plague. Co-operation could no more be done from a distance than fighting it. If the invaders had come to fight the plague, they'd have sent their best medical men to help. If they came to assist it, they'd have sent butchers, but they'd also send the very best man they had to make sure that nothing went wrong with the plague itself. The logical man to be field director of the extermination project would be the man who'd worked out the plague himself." He paused again, and said icily, "I'm no judge to pass on anybody's guilt or innocence or fate, but as a Med Service man I've authority to take measures against health hazards!"

He began to press the plunger of the filter, judging by the wavering light of the torch. The piston was itself the filter, and on one side a clear, mobile liquid began very slowly to appear.

"Just to be sure, though—you said there was a lab in the city and the doctors found nothing."

"Nothing," agreed Kim hopelessly. "There'd been a complete bacteriological survey of the planet. Nothing new appeared. Everybody's oral and intestinal flora were normal. Naturally, no alien bug would be able to compete with the strains we humans have been living with for thousands of years. So there wasn't anything unknown in any culture from any patient."

"There could have been a mutation," said Calhoun. He watched the clear serum increase. "But if your doctors couldn't pass the disease—"

"They could!" said Kim bitterly. "A massive shot of assorted bugs would pass it, breathed or swallowed or smeared on the skin. Experimental animals could be given the plague. But no one organism could be traced as giving it. No pure culture would!"

Calhoun continued to watch the clear fluid develop on the delivery side of the filter piston. Presently there was better than twelve cubic centimeters of clear serum on one side, and an almost solid block of clumped blood cells on the other. He drew off the transparent fluid with a fine precision.

"We're working under far from asceptic conditions," he said wryly, "but we have to take the chances. Anyhow, I'm getting a hunch. A pathogenic mechanism that isn't a single, identifiable bug—it's not natural. It smells of the laboratory, just as uniformed murderers who are immune to a plague do. It's not too wild a guess to suspect that somebody worked out the plague as well as the immunization of the invaders. That it was especially designed to baffle the doctors who might try to fight it."

"It did," agreed Kim bitterly.

"So," said Calhoun, "maybe a pure culture wouldn't carry the plague. Maybe the disaster-producing apparatus simply isn't there when you make pure cultures. There's even a reason to suspect something specific. Murgatroyd was a very sick animal. I've only known of one previous case in which a *tormal* reacted as violently as Murgatroyd did to an injection. That case had us sweating."

"If I were going to live," said Kim grimly, "I might ask what it was."

"Since you're going to," Calhoun told him, "I'll tell you. It was a pair of organisms. Separately, they were so near harmless as makes no difference. Together, their toxins combined to be pure poison. It was synergy. They were a synergic pair which, together, were like high explosive. That one was the devil to track down!"

He went back across the glade. Murgatroyd came skipping after him, scratching at the anesthetic patch on his side.

"You go first," said Calhoun briefly to Helen Jons. "This is an antibody serum. You may itch afterward, but I doubt it. Your arm, please."

She bared her pitifully thin arm. He gave her practically a cc of fluid which—plus blood corpuscles and some forty-odd other essential substances—had been circulating in Murgatroyd's bloodstream not long since. The blood corpuscles had been clumped and removed by one compound plus the filter, and the anticoagulant had neatly modified most of the others. In a matter of minutes, the lab kit had prepared as usable a serum as any animal-using technique would produce. Logically, the antibodies it contained should be isolated and their chemical structure determined. They should be synthesized, and the synthetic antibody-complex administered to plague victims. But Calhoun faced a group of people doomed to die. He could only use his field kit to produce a small-scale miracle for them. He could not do a mass-production job.

"Next!" said Calhoun. "Tell them what it's all about, Kim."

The gaunt young man bared his own arm. "If what he says is so, this will cure us. If it isn't so, nothing can do us any more harm."

And Calhoun briskly gave them, one after another, the shots of what ought to be a curative serum for an unidentified disease which he suspected was not caused by any single germ, but by a partnership. Synergy is an acting together. Charcoal will burn quietly. Liquid air will not burn at all. But the two together constitute a violent explosive. The ancient simple drug sulfa is not intoxicating. A glass of wine is not intoxicating. But the two together have the kick of dynamite. Synergy in medicine is a process by which,

when one substance with one effect is given in combination
with another substance with another effect, the two together
have the consequences of a third substance intensified to
fourth or fifth or tenth power.

"I think," said Calhoun when he'd finished, "that by
morning you'll feel better—perhaps cured of the plague entirely and only weak from failure to force yourselves to take
nourishment. If it turns out that way, then I advise you all
to get as far away from the city as possible for a considerable
while. I think this planet is going to be repopulated. I suspect that shiploads of colonists are on the way here now, but
not from Dettra, which built the city. And I definitely guess
that, sick or well, you're going to be in trouble if or when
you contact the new colonists."

They looked tiredly at him. They were a singular lot of
people. Each one seemed half-starved, yet their eyes had
not the brightness of suffering. They looked weary beyond
belief, and yet there was no self-neglect. They were of that
singular human type which maintains human civilization
against the inertia of the race, because it drives itself to
get needed things done. It is not glamorous, this dogged
part of mankind which keeps things going. It is sometimes
absurd. For dying folk to wash themselves when even such
exertion calls for enormous resolution is not exactly rational.
To help each other try to die with dignity was much more
a matter of self-respect than of intellectual decision. But as
a Med Ship man, Calhoun viewed them with some warmth.
They were the type that has to be called on when an emergency occurs and the wealth-gathering type tends to flee
and the low-time-sense part of a population inclines to riot
or loot or worse.

Now they waited listlessly for their own deaths.

"There's no exact precedent for what's happened here,"
explained Calhoun. "A thousand years or so ago there was a
king of France—a country back on old Earth—who tried to
wipe out a disease called leprosy by executing all the people
who had it. But lepers were a nuisance. They couldn't work.
They had to be fed by charity. They died in inconvenient
places and only other lepers dared handle their bodies.

They tended to throw normal human life out of kilter. That wasn't the case here. The man I killed wanted you dead for another reason. He and his friends wanted you dead right away."

The gaunt Kim Walpole said tiredly:

"He wanted to dispose of our bodies in a sanitary fashion."

"Nonsense!" snapped Calhoun. "The city's infected. You lived, ate, breathed, walked in it. Nobody can dare use that city unless they know how the contagion's transmitted, and how to counteract it. Your own colonists turned back. These men wouldn't have landed if they hadn't known they were safe!"

There was silence.

"If the plague is an intended crime," added Calhoun, "you are the witnesses to it. You've got to be gotten rid of before colonists from somewhere other than Dettra arrive here."

The dark-bearded man growled:

"Monstrous! Monstrous!"

"Agreed," said Calhoun. "But there's no interstellar government now, any more than there was a planetary government in the old days back on Earth. So if somebody pirates a colony ready to be occupied, there's no authority able to throw them out. The only recourse would be war. And nobody is going to start an interplanetary war—not with the bombs that can be landed! If the invaders can land a population here, they can keep it here. It's piracy, with nobody able to do anything to the pirates." He paused, and said with irony, "Of course they could be persuaded that they were wrong."

But that was not even worth thinking about. In the computation of probabilities in human conduct, self-interest is a high-value factor. Children and barbarians have clear ideas of justice due *to* them, but no idea at all of justice due *from* them. And though human colonies spread toward the galaxy's rim, there was still a large part of every population which was civilized only in that it could use tools. Most people still remained comfortably barbaric or childish in their emotional lives. It was a fact that had to be considered in Calhoun's profession. It bore remarkably on matters of contagion, and health, and life itself.

"You'll have to hide. Perhaps permanently," he told them. "It depends partly on what happens to me, however, I have to go into the city. There's a very serious health problem there."

Kim said with irony:

"In the city? Everybody's healthy there. There're so healthy that they come out to hunt us down for sport!"

"Considering that the city's thoroughly infected, their immunity is a health problem," said Calhoun. "But besides that, it looks like the original cause of the plague is there, too. I'd guess that the originator of this plague is technical director of the exterminating operation that's in progress on this planet. I'd guess he's in the ship that brought the butcher-invaders. I'd be willing to bet that he's got a very fine laboratory on the ship."

Kim stared at him. He clenched and unclenched his hands.

"And I'd say it ought to be quite useless to fight this plague before that man and that laboratory were taken care of," said Calhoun. "You people are probably all right. I think you'll wake up feeling better. You may be well. But if the plague is artificial, if it was developed to make a colony planet useless to the world that built it, but healthy for people who want to sieze it . . ."

"What?"

"It may be the best plague that was developed for the purpose, but you can be sure it's not the only one. Dozens of strains of deadly bugs would have to be developed to be sure of getting the deadliest. Different kinds of concealment would have to be tried, in case somebody guessed the synergy trick, as I did, and could do something about the first plague used. There'd have to be a second and third and fourth plague available. You see?"

Kim nodded, speechless.

"A setup like that is a real health hazard," said Calhoun. "As a Med Service man, I have to deal with it. It's much more important than your life or mine or Murgatroyd's. So I have to go into the city to do what can be done. Meanwhile, you'd better lie down now. Give Murgatroyd's antibodies a chance to work."

Kim started to move away. Then he said:

"You've been exposed. Have you protected yourself?"

"Give me a quarter-cc shot," said Calhoun. "That should do."

He handed the injector to the gaunt young man. He noted the deftness with which Kim handled it. Then he helped get the survivors of the original group—there were six of them now— to the leafy beds under the shelters. They were very quiet, even more quiet than their illness demanded. They were very polite. The old man and woman who'd struggled back to the glade together made a special effort to bid Calhoun good night with the courtesy appropriate to city folk of tradition.

Calhoun settled down to keep watch through the night. Murgatroyd snuggled confidingly close to him. There was silence.

But not complete silence. The night of Maris III was filled with tiny noises, and some not so faint. There were little squeaks which seemed to come from all directions, including overhead. There were chirpings which were definitely at ground level. There was a sound like effortful grunting in the direction of the hills. In the lowlands there was a rumbling which moved very slowly from one place to another. By its rate of motion, Calhoun guessed that a pack or herd of small animals was making a night journey and uttering deep-bass noises as it traveled.

He debated certain grim possibilities. The man he'd killed had had a ground-car key in his pocket. He'd probably come out in a powered vehicle. He might have had a companion, and the method of hunting down fugitives—successful, in his case—was probably well established. That companion might come looking for him, so watchfulness was necessary.

Meanwhile, there was the plague. The idea of synergy was still most plausible. Suppose the toxins—the poisonous metabolic products— of two separate kinds of bacteria combined to lessen the ability of the blood to carry oxygen and scavenge away carbon dioxide? It would be extremely difficult to identify the pair, and the symptoms would be accounted for. No pure culture of any organism to be found would give the plague. Each, by itself, would be harmless. Only a combination of the two would be injurious. And if so much was assumed, and the blood lost its capacity to carry oxygen, mental listlessness would be the first symptom of all. The brain requires a high oxygen level in its blood supply if it is to work properly. Let a man's brain be gradually, slowly, starved of oxygen and all the noted effects would follow. His other organs would slow down, but at a lesser rate. He would not remember to eat. His blood would still digest food and burn away its own fat,—though more and more sluggishly, while his brain worked only foggily. He would become only semiconscious, and then there would come a time of coma when unconsciousness claimed him and his body lived on only as an idling machine, until it ran out of fuel and died.

Calhoun tried urgently to figure out a synergic combination which might make a man's blood cease to do its work. Perhaps only minute quantities of the dual poison might be needed. It might work as an antivitamin or an antienzyme, or—

The invaders of the city were immune, though. Quite possibly the same antibodies Murgatroyd had produced were responsible for their safety. Somewhere, somebody had very horribly used the science of medicine to commit a monstrous crime. But medicine was still a science. It was still a body of knowledge of natural law. And natural laws are consistent and work together toward that purpose for which the universe was made.

He heard a movement across the clearing. He reached for his blaster. Then he saw what the motion was. It was Kim Walpole, intolerably weary, trudging with infinite effort to where Helen Jons lay. Calhoun heard him ask heavily:

"You're all right?"

"Yes, Kim," said the girl softly. "I couldn't sleep. I'm wondering if we can hope."

Kim did not answer.

"If we live . . ." said the girl yearningly. She stopped.

Calhoun felt that he ought to put his fingers in his ears. The conversation was strictly private. But he needed to be on guard, so he coughed, to give notice that he heard. Kim called to him:

"Calhoun?"

"Yes," said Calhoun. "If you two talk, I suggest that you do it in whispers. I'm going to watch in case the man I killed had a companion who might come looking for him. One question, though. If the plague is artificial, it had to be started. Did a ship land here two weeks or a month before your workmen began to be ill? It could have come from anywhere."

"There was no landing of any ship," said Kim. "No."

Calhoun frowned. His reasoning seemed airtight. The plague must have been introduced here from somewhere else!

"There had to be," he insisted. "Any kind of ship! From anywhere!"

"There wasn't," repeated Kim. "We had no off-planet communication for three months before the plague appeared. There's been no ship here at all except from Dettra, with supplies and workmen and that sort of thing."

Calhoun scowled. This was impossible. Then Helen's voice sounded very faintly. Kim made a murmurous response. Then he said:

"Helen reminds me that there was a queer roll of thunder one night not long before the plague began. She's not sure it means anything, but in the middle of the night, with all the stars shining, thunder rolled back and forth across the sky above the city. This was a week or two before the plague. It waked everybody. Then it rolled away to the horizon and beyond. The weather people had no explanation for it."

Calhoun considered. Murgatroyd nestled still closer to him. He snapped his fingers suddenly.

"That was it!" he said savagely. "That's the trick! I haven't all the answers, but I know some very fine questions to ask now. And I think I know where to ask them."

He settled back. Murgatroyd slept. There was the faintest

possible murmur of voices where Kim Walpole and the girl Helen talked wistfully of the possibility of hope.

Calhoun contemplated the problem before him. There were very, very few survivors of the people who belonged in the city. There was a shipload of murderers—butchers!—who had landed to see that the last of them were destroyed. Undoubtedly there was a highly trained and probably brilliant microbiologist in the invaders' expedition. One would be needed, to make sure of the success of the plague and to verify the absolute protection of the butchers, so that other colonists could come here to take over and use the planet. There could be no failure of protection for the people *not* of Dettra who expected to inhabit this world. There would have to be completely competent supervision of this almost unthinkable, this monstrous stealing of a world.

"The plague would probably be a virus pair," muttered Calhoun. "Probably introduced and scattered by a ship with wings *and* rockets. It'd have wings because it wouldn't want to land, but did want to sweep back and forth over the city. It'd drop frozen pellets of the double virus culture. They'd drop down toward the ground, melting and evaporating as they fell, and they'd flow over the city as an invisible, descending blanket of contagion coating everything. Then the ship would head away over the horizon and out to space on its rockets. Its wings wouldn't matter out of atmosphere and it'd go into overdrive and go back home to wait . . ."

He felt an icy anger, more savage than any rage could be. With this technique, a confederation of human beings utterly without pity could become parasitic on other worlds. They could take over any world by destroying its people, and no other people could make any effective protest, because the stolen world would be useless except to the murderers who had taken it over. This affair on Maris III might be merely a test of the new ruthlessness. The murderer-planet could spread its ghastly culture like a cancer through the galaxy.

But there were two other things involved beside a practise of conquest through murder by artificial plagues. One was what would happen to the people—the ordinary, common-place citizens—of a civilization which spread and subsisted by such means. It would not be good for them. In the aggregate, they'd be worse off than the people who died.

The other?

"They might make a field test of their system," said Calhoun very coldly," without doing anything more serious to the Med Service than killing one man—me—and destroying one small Med Ship. But they couldn't adopt this system on any sort of scale without destroying the Med Service first. I'm beginning to dislike this business excessively!"

CHAPTER V

"Very much of physical science is merely the comprehension of long-observed facts. In human conduct there is a long tradition of observation, but a very brief record of comprehension. For example, human lives in contact with other human lives follow the rules of other ecological systems. All too often, however, a man imagines that an ecological system is composed only of things, whereas such a system operates through the actions of things. It is not possible for any part of an ecological complex to act upon the other parts without being acted upon in its turn. So that it follows that it is singularly stupid—but amazingly common—for an individual to assume human society to be passive and unreactive. He may assume that he can do what he pleases, but inevitably there is a reaction as energetic as his action, and as well-directed. Moreover, probability . . ."

Probability and Human Conduct——Fitzgerald

AN HOUR after sunrise Calhoun's shoulder pack was empty of food. The refugees arose, and they were weak and ravenous. Their respiration had slowed to normal. Their pulses no longer pounded. Their eyes were no longer dull, but very bright. But they were in advanced states of malnutrition, and now were aware of it. Their brains were again receiving adequate oxygen and their metabolism was at normal level—and they knew they were starving.

Calhoun served as cook. He trudged to the spring that Helen described. He brought back water. While they sucked on sweet tablets from his rations and watched with hungry eyes, he made soup from the dehydrated rations he'd carried for Murgatroyd and himself. He gave it to them as the first thing their stomachs were likely to digest.

He watched as they fed themselves. The elderly man and woman sipped delicately, looking at each other. The man with the broad dark beard ate with tremendous self-restraint. Helen fed the weakest, oldest man, between spoonsful for herself, and Kim Walpole ate slowly, brooding.

Calhoun kept them going, slowly providing them with food, until he had no more to offer. By then they had made highly satisfying gains in strength. But it was then late morning.

He drew Kim aside.

"During the night," he said, "I got another lot of serum ready. I'm leaving it with you, with an injector. You'll find other fugitives. I gave you massive doses. You'd better be stingy. Try half-cc shots. Maybe you can skimp that."

"What about you?" demanded Kim.

Calhoun shrugged.

"I've got an awful lot of authority, if I can make it stick," he said drily. "As a Med Ship man. I've power to take complete charge of any health emergency. You people have a plague here. That's one emergency. It's artificial. That's another. The people who've spread it here have reason, in their success to date on this planet, to think they can take over any other world they choose. And, human nature being what it is, that's the biggest health hazard in history. I've got to get to work on it."

"There's a shipload of armed murderers here," said Kim.

"I'm not much interested in them," admitted Calhoun. "I want to get at the man who's at the head of this thing. As I told you, he should have other plagues in stock. It's entirely possible that the operation here is no more than a small-scale field test of a new technique for conquest."

"If those butchers find you, you'll be killed."

"True," admitted Calhoun. "But the number of chance happenings that could favor me is much greater than the number that could favor them. I'm working with nature, and they're working against it. Anyhow, as a Med Service man, I should prevent the landing of anybody—anybody at all—on a plague—stricken planet like this. And I suspect that there are plans for landings. I should set up an effective quarantine."

His tone was dry. Kim Walpole stared.

"You mean you'll try to stop them?"

"I shall try," said Calhoun, "to implement the authority vested in me by the Med Service for such cases as this. The rules about quarantine are rather strict."

"You'll be killed," said Kim again.

Calhoun ignored the repeated prediction.

"That invader found you," he observed, "because he knew that you'd have to drink. So he found a brook and followed it up, looking for signs of humans drinking from it. He found footprints about the spring. I found his footprints there, too. That's the trick you'll use to find other fugitives. But pass on the word not to leave tracks hereafter. For other advice, I advise you to get all the weapons you can. Modern ones, of course. You've got the blaster from the man I killed."

"I think," said Kim between his teeth, "that I'll get some more. If hunters from the city do track us to our drinking places, I'll know how to get more weapons!"

"Yes," agreed Calhoun. "Now. Murgatroyd made the antibodies that cured you. As a general rule, you can expect antibody production in your own bodies once an infection begins to be licked. In case of extreme emergency, each of you can probably supply antibodies for a fair number of other plague victims. You might try serum from blisters you produce on your skin. Quite often antibodies turn up there. I don't guarantee it, but sometimes it works."

He paused. Kim Walpole said harshly:

"But you! Isn't there anything we can do for you?"

"I was going to ask you something," said Calhoun. He produced the telephoto films of the city as photographed from space. "There's a laboratory in the city. A biochemistry lab. Show me where to look for it."

Walpole gave explicit directions, pointing out the spot on the photo. Calhoun nodded. Then Kim said fiercely:

"But tell us something we can do! We'll be strong, presently, and we'll have weapons. We'll track downstream to where hunters leave their ground-cars and be equipped with them. We can help you!"

Calhoun nodded approvingly.

"Right. If you see the smoke of a good-sized fire in the city, and if you've got a fair number of fairly strong men with you, and if you've got ground-cars, you might investigate. But be cagey about it. Very cagey!"

"If you signal we'll come," said Kim Walpole grimly, "no matter how few we are."

"Fine," said Calhoun. He had no intention of calling on these weakened, starving people for help.

He swung his depleted pack on his back again and slipped away from the glade. He made his way to the spring, which flowed up clear and cool from unseen depths. He headed down the little brook which flowed away from it. Murgatroyd raced along its banks. He hated to get his paws wet. Presently, where the underbrush grew thickly close to the water's edge, Murgatroyd wailed, "Chee! Chee!" Calhoun plucked him from the ground and set him on his shoulder. Murgatroyd clung blissfully there as Calhoun followed down the stream-bed. He adored being carried.

Two miles down, there was another cultivated field. This one was planted with an outsized root crop, and Calhoun walked past shoulder-high bushes with four-inch blue-and-white flowers. He recognized the plant as one of the family Solanaceae—belladona was still used in medicine—but he couldn't identify it until he dug up a root and found a tuber. But the six-pound specimen he uncovered was still too young and green to be eaten. Murgatroyd refused to touch it.

Calhoun was ruefully considering the limitations of specialized training when he came to the end of the cultivated field. There was a highway. It was new, of course. City, fields, highways and all the physical aspects of civilized life had been built on this planet before the arrival of the colonists who were to inhabit it. It was extraordinary to see such preparations for a population not yet on hand. But Calhoun was much more interested in the ground-car he found waiting on the highway, hard by a tiny bridge under which a small brook flowed.

The key he'd taken from the dead invader fitted. He got in the car and beckoned Murgatroyd to the seat beside him.

"Characters like the man I killed, Murgatroyd," he observed, "aren't very important. There're mere butchers—killers. That sort of character likes to loot. There's nothing here for them to loot. They're bound to be bored. They're bound to be restless. We won't have much trouble with them. I'm worrying about the man who possibly designed and is certainly supervising the action of the plague. I look for trouble with him."

The ground-car was in motion then, toward the city. He drove on.

It was a good twenty miles, but he did not encounter a single other vehicle. Presently the city lay spread out before him. He surveyed it thoughtfully. It was very beautiful. Fifty generations of architects on many worlds had played with stone and steel, groping for perfection. This city was a close approach. There were towers which glittered whitely, and low buildings which seemed to nestle on the vegetation-covered ground. There were soaring bridges and gracefully curving highways, and park areas laid out and ready. There was no monotony anywhere.

The only exception to gracefulness was the massive landing grid, half a mile and a mile across, which was a lace-work of monster steel girders with spider-thin wires of copper woven about them in the complex curves its operation required. Inside it, Calhoun could see the ship of the invaders. It had landed in the grid enclosure, and later Calhoun had blown out the transformers of the grid. They were probably in process of repair now. But the ship stood sturdily on the ground inside the great structure which dwarfed it.

"The man we're after will be in that ship, Murgatroyd," said Calhoun. "He'll have inner and outer lock-doors fastened, and he'll be inside a six-inch beryllium-steel wall. Rather difficult to break in upon. And he'll be uneasy. An intellectual type gone wrong doesn't feel at ease with the kind of butchers he has to associate with. I think the problem is to get him to invite us into his parlor. But it may not be simple."

"*Chee,*" said Murgatroyd doubtfully.

"Oh, we'll manage," Calhoun assured him. "Somehow!"

He spread out his photographs. Kim Walpole had marked where he should go and a route to it. Having been in the city while it was being built, he knew even the service lanes which, being sunken, were not a part of the city's good looks.

"But the invaders," explained Calhoun, "won't deign to use grubby service lanes. They consider themselves aristocrats because they were sent to be conquerors, though the work required of them was simple butchery. I wonder what sort of swine run the world they came from!"

He put away the photos and headed for the city again. He branched off the main highway, near the city. A turn-off descended into a cut. The road in the cut was intended for loads of agricultural produce entering the city. It was strictly utilitarian. It ran below the surface of the park areas, and entered the city without pride. When among the buildings it ran between rows of undecorative gates, behind which waste matter was destined to be collected to be carted away as fertilizer for the fields. The city was very well designed.

Rolling through the echoing sunken road, Calhoun saw, just once, a ground-car in motion on a far-flung, cobwebby bridge between two tall towers. It was high overhead. Nobody in it would be watching grubby commerce roads.

The whole affair was very simple indeed. Calhoun brought the car to a stop beneath the overhang of a balconied building many stories high. He got out and opened the gate. He drove the car into the cavernous, so-far-unused lower part of the building. He closed the gate behind him. He was in the center of the city, and his presence was unknown. This was at three or later in the afternoon.

He climbed a clean new flight of steps and came to the sections the public would use. There were glassy walls which changed their look as one moved between them.

There were the lifts. Calhoun did not try to use them. He led Murgatroyd up the circular ramps which led upward in case of unthinkable emergency. He and Murgatroyd plodded up and up. Calhoun kept count.

On the fifth level there were signs of use, while all the others had that dusty cleanness of a structure which has been completed but not yet occupied.

"Here we are," said Calhoun cheerfully.

But he had his blaster in his hand when he opened the door of the laboratory. It was empty. He looked approvingly about as he hunted for the storeroom. It was a perfectly equipped biological laboratory, and it had been in use. Here the few doomed physicians awaiting the city's population had worked desperately against the plague. Calhoun saw the trays of cultures they'd made, dried up and dead now. Somebody had turned over a chair. Probably when the laboratory was searched by the invaders, in case someone not of their kind still remained alive in it.

He found the storeroom. Murgatroyd watched with bright eyes as he rummaged.

"Here we have the things men use to cure each other," said Calhoun oracularly. "Practically every one a poison save for its special use! Here's an assortment of spores—pathogenic organisms, Murgatroyd. They have their uses. And here are drugs which are synthesized nowadays, but are descended from the poisons found on the spears of savages. Great helps in medicine. And here are the anesthetics—poisons too. These are what I am counting on."

He chose, very painstakingly. Dextrethyl. Polysulfate. The one marked inflammable and dangerous. The other with the maximum permissible dose on its label, and the names of counteracting substances which would neutralize it. He burdened himself. Murgatroyd reached up a paw. Since Calhoun was carrying something, he wanted to carry something too.

They went down the circular ramp again as sunset drew near. Calhoun searched once more in the below-surface levels of the buildings. He found what he wanted—a painter's vortex-gun which would throw "smoke rings" of tiny paint droplets at a wall or object to be painted. One could vary the size of the ring at impact from a bare inch to a three-foot spread.

Calhoun cleaned the paint-gun. He was meticulous about it. He filled its tank with dextrethyl brought down from the laboratory. He piled the empty containers out of sight.

"This trick," he observed, as he picked up the paint-gun again, "was devised to be used on a poor devil of a lunatic who carried a bomb in his pocket for protection against imaginary assassins. It would have devastated a quarter-mile circle, so he had to be handled gently."

He patted his pockets. He nodded.

"Now we go hunting—with an oversized atomizer loaded with dextrethyl. I've polysulfate and an injector to secure each specimen I knock over. Not too good, eh? But if I have to use a blaster I'll have failed."

He looked out a window at the sky. It was now late dusk. He went back to the gate to the service road. He went out and carefully closed it behind him. On foot, with many references to the photomaps, he began to find his way toward the landing grid. It ought to be something like the center of the invaders' location.

It was dark when he climbed other service stairs from the cellar of another building. This was the communications building of the city. It had been the key to the mopping-up process the invaders began on landing. Its callboard would show which apartments had communicators in use. When such a call showed, a murder party could be sent to take care of the caller. Even after the first night, some individual, isolated folk might remain, unaware of what was happening. So there would be somebody on watch, just in case a dying man called for the solace of a human voice while still he lived.

There was a man on watch. Calhoun saw a lighted room. Paint-gun ready, he moved very silently toward it. Murgatroyd padded faithfully behind him.

Outside the door, Calhoun adjusted his curious weapon. He entered. The man nodded in a chair before the lifeless board. When Calhoun entered he raised his head and yawned.

He turned.

Calhoun sprayed him with smoke rings—vortex rings. But the rings were spinning missiles of vaporized dextrethyl, that anesthetic developed from ethyl chloride some two hundred years before, and not yet bettered for its special uses. One of its properties was that the faintest whiff of its vapor produced a reflex impulse to gasp. A second property was that, like the ancient ethyl chloride, it was the quickest-acting anesthetic known.

The man by the callboard saw Calhoun. His nostrils caught the odor of dextrethyl. He gasped.

He fell unconscious.

Calhoun waited patiently until the dextrethyl was out of the way. It was almost unique among vapors in that at room temperature it was lighter than air. It rose toward the ceiling. Presently Calhoun moved forward and brought out the poly-sulfate injector. He bent over the unconscious man. He did not touch him otherwise.

He turned and walked out of the room with Murgatroyd piously marching behind him.

Outside, Calhoun said:

"As one medical man to another, perhaps I shouldn't have done that. But I'm dealing with a health hazard, a plague. Sometimes one has to use psychology to supplement standard measures. I consider that the case here. Anyhow this man should be missed sooner than most. He has a job where his failure to act should be noticed."

"Chee?" asked Murgatroyd zestfully.

"No," said Calhoun. "He won't die. He wouldn't be so unkind."

It was dark outdoors now. When Calhoun stepped out into the street—he'd touched nothing in the callboard office to show that he'd entered it—nightfall was complete. Stars shone brightly, but the empty, unlighted ways of the city were black. There seemed to be a formless menace in the air. When Calhoun moved down the street, Murgatroyd, who hated the dark, reached up a furry paw and held on to Calhoun's hand for reassurance.

Calhoun moved silently and Murgatroyd's footfalls were

inaudible. The feel of the never-lived-in city was appalling. A sleeping city seems ghostly and strange, even with lighted streets. An abandoned city is intolerably desolate, with all its inhabitants gone or dead. But a city which has never lived, which lies lifeless under a night sky because its people never came to occupy it—that city has the worst feeling of all. It seems unnatural. It seems insane. It is like a corpse which could have lived but never acquired a soul, and now waits horribly for something demoniac to enter it and give it a seeming of life too horrifying to imagine.

The invaders unquestionably felt that creeping atmosphere of horror. Presently there was proof. Calhoun heard small, drunken noises in the street. He tracked them cautiously. He found the place—one lighted ground-floor window on a long street lined on both sides with towering structures reaching for the sky. The sheer walls were utterly dark. The narrow lane of stars that could be seen overhead seemed utterly remote. The street itself was empty and dark, and murmurous with echoes of sounds that had not ever really been made. And here there were no natural sounds at all. Building walls cut off the normal night-sounds of the open country. There was a dead and muffled and murmurous stillness fit to crack one's eardrums.

Except for the drunken singing. Men drank together in an unnecessarily small room, which they had lighted very brightly to try to make it seem alive. All about them was deadness and stillness, so they made supposedly festive noises, priming themselves to cheerfulness with many bottles. With enough to drink, perhaps, the illusion could be believed in. But it was a pitifully tiny thread of sound in a dark and empty city. Outside, where Calhoun and Murgatroyd paused to listen, the noise of drunken singing had a quality of biting irony.

Calhoun grunted, and the sound echoed endlessly between the stark walls around and above.

"We could use those characters," he said coldly, "only there are too many of them."

He and Murgatroyd went on. He'd familiarized himself with the stars, earlier, and knew that he moved in the direction of the landing grid. He'd arranged for one man on duty—at the callboard—to fail to do his work. The process was carefully chosen. He'd knocked out the invader with vortex rings of dextrethyl vapor, and then had given him a shot of polysulphate. The combination was standard, like magnesium sulphate and ether, centuries before. Polysulphate was an assisting anesthetic, never used alone because a man who was knocked out by it stayed out for days. In surgery it was used in a quantity which seemed not to affect a man at all, yet the least whiff of dextrethyl would then put him under for an operation, while he could instantly be revived. It was safer and under better control than any other kind of anesthesia.

But Calhoun had reversed the process. He'd put the callboard operator under with vapor, and then given poly-sulphate to keep him under for sixty hours or more. And then he'd left him. When the invader was found unconscious, it would bother the other butchers very much. They'd never suspect his condition to be the result of enemy action. They'd consider him in a coma. A coma was the last effect of the plague that had presented them with a planet. They'd believe their fellow to be dying of the plague they were supposed to be immune to. They would panic, expecting immediate death for themselves. But more than one man in a comalike state would be more effective in producing complete disorganization and despair.

A door banged, back by the lighted window in the desolate black street. Someone came out. Someone else. A third man. They moved along the street, singing hoarsely and untunefully and with words as slurred and uncertain as their footsteps. Echoes resounded between the high building walls. The effect was eerie.

Calhoun moved into a doorway. He waited. When the three men were opposite him, they linked arms to steady themselves. One man roared out quite unprintable verses of a song in which another joined uncertainly from time to time. The third protested aggrievedly. He halted, and the three of them argued solemnly about something indefinable, swaying as they talked with owlish, drunken gravity.

Calhoun lifted the paint-gun. He held down the trigger.

Invisible rings of dextrethyl vapor whisked toward the trio. They gasped. They collapsed. Calhoun took his measures.

Presently one man lay unconscious on the street in a coma which imitated perfectly, except for the emaciation, the terminal coma of the fugitives from the city. Some distance away Calhoun plodded on toward the landng grid with a second man, also unconscious, over his shoulder. Murgatroyd followed closely. The third man, stripped to his underwear, waited where he might be found within the next day or two.

CHAPTER VI

"It is improper to use the term 'gambler' of a man who uses actuarial tables or tables of probability to make wagers which ensure him a favorable percentage of returns. Still less is it proper to call a man who cheats a gambler. He eliminates chance from his operations by his cheating. He does not gamble at all. 'The only true gambler is one who takes risks without considering chance; who acts upon reason or intuition or hunch or superstition without advertising to probability. He ignores the fact that chance as well as thought has a share in determining the outcome of any action. In this sense, the criminal is the true gambler. He is always confident that probability will not interfere; that no random happening will occur. To date, however, there has been no statistical analysis of a crime which has proved it an action which a reasonably prudent man would risk. The effects of pure, random happen-chance can be so overwhelming . . ."

Probability and Human Conduct——Fitzgerald

THE NIGHT NOISES of the planet Maris III came from all the open space beyond the city itself. From the buildings themselves, of course, there was only silence. There were park areas left between them here and there, and green spaces bordered all the highways. But only small chirping sounds came from the city. The open country sang to the stars.

Calhoun settled himself, with an unconscious burden and Murgatroyd. He could not know how long it would be be-

fore the callboard operator would be missed and checked
on. He was sure, though, that the appearance of terminal
coma in a man who should be immune to the plague would
produce results. The callboard man would be brought to the
microbiologist who must be in charge of this operation murder. There had to be such a man. He had to know all about
the plague. He had to be able to meet any peculiarity that
came up. At a guess, only the best qualified of all the men
who'd worked to develop the plague would be trusted with
its first field test. He might even be the man who himself
had devised the synergic combination. He'd be on hand.
He'd have every possible bit of equipment he could need,
in a superlatively arranged laboratory on the ship. And the
callboard man would be brought to him.

Calhoun waited. He had another man in seeming coma,
ready for use when the time came. Now he rested in the
deep star-shadow of one of the landing grid's massive sup-
ports. Murgatroyd stayed close to him. The *tormal* was
normally active by day. Darkness daunted him. He tended
to whimper if he could not be close to Calhoun.

Overhead loomed the soaring, heavy arches of the landing
grid. The grid should handle twenty-thousand-ton liners, and
heavier ones too. It was designed to conduct the interstellar
business of a world. Beyond it, the city reared up against
the stars. The control building, from which the grid was
operated, sprawled over half an acre, not far from where
Calhoun lay in wait. His eyes were adjusted to the darkness,
and he could see faint glows as if there were lighted windows
facing away from him. He was within a hundred yards of the
giant, globular ship which had brought the invaders here
to do their work of butchery.

There was quiet save for the chorus of myriads of small
voices which serenaded the heavens. It was a remarkable
total sound. Now and again Calhoun heard sustained deep-
bass notes, like the lowest possible tones of a great organ.
Then there were liquid trillings which might come from
any kind of bird or beast or reptile. In between came chirpings and abrupt paeans of music, like woodwinds essaying
tentative melodic runs.

It was easy for Calhoun to wait. The whole affair had added itself up in his mind. He felt that he not only knew what had happened on this world, but what might happen elsewhere if this particular enterprise proved profitable.

This world of Maris III was to have been a daughter-planet of the old, long-settled Dettra Two. There would have been a close linkage of interest and traditions between the two worlds. They would have had a common tradition, and common blood, and all the ties that can keep two civilizations akin. The older culture had built a city and farms and facilities for half a million of its more adventurous members. They would have come here and entered upon and possessed this world, and they would have zestfully begun its development in the image of the older planet. They would have proudly begun payment for what they had received, and even more proudly prepared to receive more and more and yet more of the senior world's crowded people.

All this was in accord with natural law, which not only determines the courses of worlds about their central suns, but dictates what is wise and fit and suitable for mankind. But men need not heed the laws of nature. They cannot be changed, but they can be broken. And somewhere there was a world, or at least the government of a world, which essayed to break the laws Calhoun knew were essential.

In the great cosmos even crime is matter-of-fact. Natural laws can be twisted to aid it. For example, a spaceship could be built with wings. In space they would not matter. Normally they would be useless. But if somebody wanted to commit a very great crime, a spaceship could be built with wings, and instead of entering atmosphere on rockets designed only to let it down gently in case of emergency, it could enter an unsuspecting planet's air and fly there on the wings it had brought through light-years of emptiness.

Such a winged spacecraft, flying by rocket power as an airplane, could dump out frozen pellets of contagion. It could choose a place for this dumping which was upwind from a city, and it could choose a height so that an area of many, many square miles would be saturated with invisible, deadly creators of disease. The ship could even fly away and up and up and up, and ultimately depend on its rockets alone in airlessness to take it up to where its spacedrive could operate in unstressed space. It could return to its home in overdrive, and the only sign of its coming anywhere—the only sign that would be known—would be a memory of thunder rolling in a star-filled sky. But later there would be a plague.

Exactly this had happened here. The empty city had been drenched with virus particles so tiny that only electron microscopes could tell that they existed, and could not tell them from others closely kin to them. But they were deadly. Singly, no. Alone, each of two types might produce only the most trivial of infections. Combined, they produced a toxin which took from human blood its power to carry oxygen. In a sense, the effect was like that of carbon monoxide. More directly, they caused bodies to starve for oxygen.

And all this was unnatural. Men had devised the plague and the means of spreading it. They made use of it. On the world where thunder had rolled in a cloudless sky, men and women died. Presently a ship came to verify it, to make sure that everything went wrong on Maris III. They knew the plague could not harm them. They murdered the few survivors in the city that they could find. They hunted down the others in the open country.

They now waited for more of their own kind to come, to occupy the planet made ready for them. When ships came from Dettra Two, which had built the city and prepared the fields, the settlers then in occupation could refuse to let them land. Or they could let them land and then watch them die. Maris III was useless now to the world that had developed it. Only the world that had murdered its first small population could have any benefit from it at all. Because, of course, the emigrants from the criminal world could be immunized to the plague their rulers had sent before them. They could live there freely, like the butchers who came first of all. It might seem a very brilliant course of conduct.

But Calhoun ground his teeth. He could see other angles to this affair. Men who could arrange this could go further. Much further. What he'd imagined was trivial compared to what could come next.

There was a light in motion in the city. Calhoun sat up, all alertness, to watch it. It was a ground-car on a highway, headlights glaring to light the way before it. It vanished behind buildings. It reappeared. It crossed a far-flung bridge and vanished again, and again reappeared. It was drawing closer, and presently its lights glared in Calhoun's eyes as it sped furiously across the landing grid's turf floor, headed for the sprawling building where the transformers and the controls for the grid were housed.

There it came to a swiftly braked stop. Its lights stayed on. Men jumped from it and ran into the control building. Calhoun heard no voices. The songs of the night creatures would have blotted out human voices. In minutes, though, more men came out of the building. They clustered about the ground-car. After only seconds, the car was again in motion, jouncing and bouncing over the turf toward the grounded spaceship.

It stopped within a hundred yards of where Calhoun had concealed himself. The headlights glittered and glistened against the bulging, silvery metal of the spacecraft. A man shouted at it:

"Open up! Open up! Something's happened! A man's sick! It looks like the plague!"

There was no sign. He shouted again. Another man pounded on the thick metal of the airlock's outer door.

A voice spoke suddenly out of external loud-speakers.

"What's this? What's the matter?"

Many voices tried to babble, but a harsh voice silenced them and barked statements, every one of which Calhoun could have written down in advance. There'd been a man on watch in the city's communication center. He didn't put through calls from different places in use by the invaders. Someone went to find out why. The man at the callboard was unconscious. It looked like he had the plague. It looked like the shots he'd had to make him immune didn't work.

The voice coming over the loud-speakers said:

"Nonsense! Bring him in!"

Seconds later the airlock door cracked open and descended

outward, making a ramp from the ground to the cubbyhole which was the lock as now revealed. The men on the ground hauled a limp figure out of the ground-car. They half-carried and half-dragged it up the ramp into the lock. Calhoun saw the inner door open. They dragged the figure inside.

Then nothing happened, except that one man came out almost immediately, wiping his hands on his uniform as if hysterically afraid that by touching his unconscious companion he'd infected himself with the plague.

Presently another man came out. He trembled. Then the others. The harsh voice said savagely:

"So he's got to find out what's the matter. It *can't* be the plague. We had shots against it. It's bound to be all right. Maybe he fainted or something. Stop acting like you're going to die! Go back on duty! I'll order a roll call, just in case."

Calhoun listened with satisfaction. The inner airlock door closed, but the outer one remained down as a ramp. The car trundled away, stopped and discharged some passengers at the control building, and went off into the distance. It disappeared on the highway where it had first appeared.

"The man I knocked out," he said dryly to Murgatroyd, "impresses them unfavorably. They hope he's only an accident. We'll see. But that authoritative person is going to order a roll call. He ought to find something to bother them all, when that takes place."

"*Chee,*" said Murgatroyd in a subdued tone.

There was again silence and stillness save for the open country song to the stars. There seemed to be occasional drumbeats in that chorus now.

It was half an hour before light showed on the ground by the control building. It was as if invisible doors had been opened, and light streamed out of them. In minutes a traveling light appeared. It vanished and was again visible, like the lights of the first car.

"Ha!" said Calhoun, gratified. "Checking up, they found the invader we left in the street. They reported it by communicator. Maybe they reported two others missing—one of whom is beside you, Murgatroyd. They ought to feel slightly upset."

The car dashed across the landing grid's center and braked. Figures waited for it. With the briefest of pauses it came again to the ship with the opened airlock door. The harsh voice panted:

"Here's another one! We're bringing him in."

The loud-speaker said, somehow vexedly:

"*Very well. But the first man hasn't got the plague. His metabolic rate is normal. He has not got the plague!*"

"Here's another one, just the same!"

The figures struggled up the ramp with a second limp burden. Minutes later they emerged again.

"He didn't get that first man awake," said an uneasy voice. "That looks bad to me."

"He says it ain't the plague."

"If he says it's not," snapped the authoritative voice, "then it's not! He ought to know. He invented the plague!"

Calhoun, behind the giant support for the landing grid, said, "Ah!" very quietly to himself.

"But—look here," said a frightened voice. "There were doctors in the city when we got here. Maybe some of 'em got away. Maybe—maybe they had some kinda germ that they've turned loose to kill us . . ."

The authoritative voice snarled. All the voices broke into a squabbling babble. The invaders were worried. They were frightened. Normally it would never have occurred to them to suspect a disease deliberately introduced among them. But they were here to follow up just such a disease. They did not understand such menaces. They'd been willing enough to profit, so long as the matter was strictly one-sided. But now it looked like some disease was striking them down. It seemed very probable that it was the plague to which they had been assured that they were immune. Some of them already had the shakes.

The car went away from the grounded spaceship. It stopped for a long time before the control building. There was agitated argument there. Calhoun heard the faint squabbling sound above the voices of the night. The car went away again.

He allowed twenty minutes to pass. They seemed very

long to him. Then he picked up the man he'd knocked out, outside the room with the noisy drinking party. He heaved him over his shoulder. He'd pulled the uniform of the third of his dark-street victims over his own, and that third man lay in an areaway in his underwear. He'd be found eventually.

"We'll ask for our invitation into the ship—and the laboratory, Murgatroyd. Come along!"

He moved toward the still and silent spaceship.

It swelled and loomed enormously as he approached it. The outside lock door still lay extended downward as a ramp. He tramped up on the metal incline. He went into the lock. There he banged on the inner door and called:

"Here's another one! Out like the others! What'll I do with him?"

There'd be microphones in the lock, as there were outside. But his voice wouldn't go so loudly to the control building. He could not plausibly moderate his tone. He made it agitated.

"Here's a third man, out like the others! What'll I do with him?"

A metallic voice said angrily:

"Wait!"

Calhoun waited. Two unconscious n en, brought separately by a group of men who were more frightened the second time than the first, made it extremely likely that a third unconscious man would not have a group of solicitous companions with him. One man to risk the supposed contagion was very much more likely.

He heard footsteps beyond the inner lock door. It opened A voice rasped:

"Bring him in!"

He turned his back, this man who had come down to the airlock to spring the catch of the inner door. Calhoun followed him inside the ship, with Murgatroyd trodding fearfully between his feet. The lock door clicked shut. The figure in the white lab coat went trudging on ahead. It was a small figure. It limped a little. It was not well-shaped.

Calhoun, with an unconscious member of the invading party used as a drape to hide his paint-gun—so suitable a weapon, as it had turned out up to now—followed after him. He listened grimly for any sound which would indicate any other human being inside the space ship. Now that he had seen—even from behind—the figure of the field director of the project to exterminate the proper inhabitants of Maris III, he coldly reasoned that there would probably not be even a laboratory assistant.

The queer figure moving before him fitted in a specific niche. There are people who, because they are physically unattractive, become personalities. All too many girls—and men, too—do not bother to become anything but good to look at. Some people who are not good to look at accept the situation courageously and become people who are good to know. But others rebel bitterly.

Knowing, as he did, that this man had used brains and skill and tedious labor to devise a method of mass murder, Calhoun felt almost able to write his biography. He had been grotesque. He hated those who found him grotesque. He dreamed grandiose dreams of gaining power so that he could punish those he envied and hated. He put into his schemes for revenge against a cosmos that gave him scorn, all the furious energy that could have been used in other ways. He would develop an astounding patience and an incredible venom. He would scheme and scheme and scheme . . .

Calhoun had met people who could have chosen this way. One of the great men at Sector Headquarters, whose praise was more valued than fine gold, was odd to look at when you first glimpsed him. But you never noticed it after five minutes. There was a planetary president in Cygnus, a teacher on Cetis Alpha, a musician . . . Calhoun could think of many. But the hobbling figure before him hadn't chosen to follow the natural law, which advises courage. He'd chosen hate instead, and frustration was inevitable.

Into the laboratory. Here Murgatroyd cheered. This place was brightly lighted. Gleaming instruments were familiar. Even the smells of a beautifully equipped biological laboratory were reassuring and homelike to Murgatroyd. He said happily:

"Chee-chee-chee!"

The small figure whirled. Dark eyes widened and glared.

Calhoun slipped his burden to the floor. His Med Service uniform appeared beneath the invader's tunic as the downward-sliding body tugged at the cloth.

"I'm sorry," said Calhoun gently, "but I have to put you under arrest for violating the basic principles of public health. Contriving and spreading a lethal plague amounts to at least that."

The figure whirled. It snatched. Then it darted toward Calhoun, desperately trying to use a surgeon's scalpel, the only deadly weapon within reach.

Calhoun pressed the trigger of the vortex-ring apparatus which was designed to paint the walls of buildings. Only this one didn't have paint in it. It shot invisible vortex rings of dextrethyl vapor instead.

CHAPTER VII

"In one perfectly real sense, all motives and all satisfactions are subjective. After all, we do live in our own skulls. But a man can do something he wishes to do and then contemplate the consequences of his action with pleasure. This pleasure, to be sure, is subjective, but it is directly related to reality and to the objective cosmos about him. However, there is an ultrasubjective type of motivation and satisfaction which is of great importance in human conduct. Many persons find their greatest satisfaction in contemplating themselves in some particular context. Such people find apparently complete satisfaction in a dramatic gesture, in a finely stated aspiration, or simply in a mere pretense of significance or wisdom or worth. The objective results of such gestures or pretenses are rarely considered. Very often great hardship and suffering and even deaths have been brought about by some person who raptly contemplated the beautiful drama of his behavior, and did not even think of its consequences to someone else. . . ."

Probability and Human Conduct——Fitzgerald

CALHOUN MADE the small man helpless with the invader's uniform he'd pulled over his own, and now tore it into strips.

He was painstaking about the job. He tied his captive in a
chair, and then encased him in a veritable cocoon of cloth
strips. Then he examined the laboratory.

Murgatroyd strutted as Calhoun went over the equipment.
Most of it was totally familiar. There were culture trays,
visual and electron microscopes, autoclaves and irradiation
apparatus, pipettes and instruments for microanalysis, ther-
mostatic cabinets capable of keeping culture material within
the hundredth of a degree of desired temperature. Murgatroyd was completely at home now.

Presently Calhoun heard a gasp. He turned and nodded to
his prisoner.

"How-do," he said politely. "I've been very much interested
in your work. I'm Med Service, by the way. I came here to
do a routine planetary health-check and somebody tried to
kill me when I called for landing co-ordinates. They'd have
done better to let me land and then blast me when I came
out of my ship. The other was the more dramatic gesture,
of course."

Dark, beady eyes regarded him. They changed remarkably
from moment to moment. At one instant they were filled with
a flaming fury which was practically madness. At another
they seemed to grow cunning. Yet again they showed animal-
like fear.

Calhoun said detachedly:

"I doubt that there's any use in talking to you now. I'll
wait until you have the situation figured out. I'm in the ship.
There appears to be nobody else in a condition to start any
trouble. The two men your—ah—mop-up party brought here
are out for some days." He added explanatorily, "Polysulphate.
An overdose. It's so simple I didn't think you'd guess it. I
knocked them out so you'd be ready to let me in with a
third specimen."

The mummylike bound figure made inarticulate noises.
There was the sound of grinding teeth. There were bubbling
sounds of crazy, frustrated rage.

"You're in a state of emotional shock," said Calhoun. "I
guess that part is real and part is faked. I'll leave you alone
to get over it. I want some information. I think you'll want

to bargain. I'll leave you alone to work it out."

He went out of the laboratory. He felt an acute distaste
for the man he'd captured. It was true that he believed the
small man had received an acute emotional shock on finding
himself captured and helpless. But a part of that shock
would be rage so horrible as to threaten madness. Calhoun
guessed coldly that anyone who had made the decision
and lived the life he ascribed to the bound man—his guess,
as it happened, was remarkably exact—could literally be
goaded to death or madness, now that he was bound and
could be taunted at will. It happened that he did not want
to taunt his prisoner.

He went over the ship. He checked its type and design,
verified the spaceyard in which it had been built, made an
exact list in his own mind of what would be needed to make
it into an inert hulk of no use to anybody, and then went
back to the laboratory.

His prisoner panted, exhausted. There were very minor
stretchings of the cloth strips which held him. Calhoun matter-
of-factly made them tight again. His prisoner spat unspeak-
able, hysterical curses at him.

"Good," said Calhoun, unmoved. "Get the madness out
of your system and we'll talk."

He moved to leave the laboratory again. A voice came
out of a loud-speaker, and he instantly searched for and
found the microphone by which it could be answered. He
flicked it off as his prisoner tried to scream commands into it.

"*Haven't you found out yet?*" asked the loudspeaker ap-
prehensively. "*Don't you know what's the matter with those
men? There are two more missing on roll call. There's something like panic building up. The men are guessing that a
native doctor's spreading a plague among us!*"

Calhoun shrugged. The voice came from outside. It had
been an authoritative voice, not long since. Now it was a
badly worried one. He did not answer its questions. It repeated them. It waited and asked again. It almost pleaded
for a reply. With the microphone off, however, there could
be none. Calhoun listened detachedly when the authoritative
voice, which must be that of the commander of the butchers,

grew resentful at being ignored. It faded out, trembling, shaking a little, but whether with hatred or terror he could not be sure. It could be either.

"Your popularity's diminishing," said Calhoun. He put down the microphone, safely off. He noted a spacephone receiver alongside the speaker-amplifier. "Hm," he said. "Suspicious, eh? You didn't even trust the skipper. Had to do your own receiving. Typical!"

The trussed-up, wizened man spoke suddenly with absolute cold precision.

"What do you want?" he demanded.

"Information," said Calhoun.

"For yourself? What do you want? I can give it to you!" said the mouth beneath the half-mad dark eyes. "I can give you anything you can imagine! I can give you riches more than you can dream!"

Calhoun sat negligently on the arm of a chair.

"I'll listen," he observed. "But apparently you're only technical director of the operation here. It's not a very big operation. You'd only a thousand people to kill. You're acting under orders. How could you give me anything important?"

"This—" His prisoner cursed. "This is a test—an experiment! Let me go, let it be finished, and I can give you a world to rule. I'll make you king of a planet! You'll have millions of slaves! You'll have women by hundreds or thousands if you choose!"

Calhoun said detachedly, "You wouldn't expect me to believe that without the details."

The dark eyes flamed. Then, with an effort of will that was as violent as his rage had been, the small bound figure brought itself to composure. It was not calmness. Fury surged up when he attempted a persuasive gesture and could not move. Frustration maddened him to panting for breath. But between such moments, he talked with a terrifying plausibility, with a precision of detail that showed a scheme worked out with infinite care. It was *his* scheme. He had convinced a planetary government to try it. He was necessary to it. He would have power to spare and he could bribe Calhoun with everything that was rich and alluring and apparently irresistible. He set persuasively to work to bribe him.

It was quite horrible.

First there had to be explanation, in such detail that a Med Service man could know that his bribes would infallibly be available and could not fail.

The taking-over of Maris III was, as Calhoun had more than guessed, a mere field trial of a new method for interplanetary war and conquest. Here was a new planet. It had a small caretaker population waiting for the hundreds of thousands of permanent inhabitants due to take over its ready-built city and roads and farms. It had been used for the testing of a new and irresistible kind of conquest. Plague! Plague had been rained upon its principal and, so far, only city. In the night. The people knew nothing about it. They began to die, and even then did not know why they died or what had caused it or when the cause of their deaths was introduced. They died!

Calhoun nodded. He was not impressed by the mysterious phrasing. It might have been imposing to somebody who had not worked out for himself how the plague had been introduced and what it was and how it had been designed to escape detection by ordinary microbiological methods.

His captive went on. His tone wheedled, and was strident, and in turn was utterly convincing and remarkably persuasive.

Once Maris III was occupied by colonists from the world that had sent the plague, nothing could be done. Dettra Two could never land its people in the city. They would die. Only the usurping population could survive there. For all time to come the world of Maris III must belong to the folk who had planted it with death. The permanent colonists here must be immunized like the members of the invading party themselves.

"Who," said Calhoun, "are not as happy as they used to be."

His captive licked his lips and went on, his eyes deadly and his tone reasonable and seductive and remarkably hypnotic.

But Maris III was only a test. Once the process was proved here, there were other worlds to be taken over. Not only new colony-worlds like this. Old and established worlds would find themselves attacked by plagues their doctors would be helpless to combat. Then there would come ships from the world that had tried out its technique on Maris III. The ships could end the plagues. They would prove it. They would offer to sell life to all the citizens of the dying worlds—at a price.

"Unprofessional," said Calhoun, "but probably profitable."

The price, in effect, would be submission. It would amount to slavery. Those who would not accept the bargain would die.

"Of course," said Calhoun, "they might try to back out of such a bargain later."

His captive smiled a thin-lipped smile, while his eyes did not change at all. He explained convincingly that if there was a revolt, it would not matter. The countermeasure to a new defiance would always be a new plague. There were many plagues ready to use. They would build an interstellar empire in which rebellion would be a form of suicide. No world once taken over could ever free itself. No world once chosen could possibly resist. There would be worlds by tens and scores and hundreds, to be ruled by men like Calhoun. He would rate a planet-kingdom of his own. His Med Service training entitled him to an empire! He would be absolute ruler and absolute master of millions of abject slaves who must please his most trivial whim or die!

"An objection," said Calhoun. "You haven't mentioned the Med Service. I don't think it would take kindly to such a system of planetary conquest."

Here was the highest test of the prisoner's ability to sway and persuade and convince and almost to hypnotize. He had in a matter of minutes to make the Med Service ridiculous, and to point out the defenselessness of its Sector Headquarters, and then—without arousing ancient prejudices—to make it seem natural and inevitable and almost humorous that Med Service Sector Headquarters would receive special precautionary fusion-bomb treatment as soon as the Maris III task was finished. Calhoun stirred. His prisoner spoke even more urgently, more desperately. He pictured worlds

on which every living being would be Calhoun's slave—
"That'll do," said Calhoun. "I've got the information I
wanted."

"Then release me," said his prisoner eagerly. And then his
burning eyes read Calhoun's no-longer-guarded expression.
"You accept," he cried fiercely. "You accept! You *can't*
refuse! *You can't!*"

"Of course I can," said Calhoun annoyedly. "You've no
idea! I wouldn't want a million slaves, or even one. I'm
reasonably sane! And such a crazy scheme couldn't work
anyhow. Sheer probability would throw in so many unfavorable chance happenings that it would be bound to go smash.
I'm proof of it. I'm an unfavorable chance happening right
here, the very first time you try the beastly business!"

His prisoner tried to talk more persuasively still. He tried
to be more tempting still. He tried, but his throat clicked.
He struggled to be more convincing and more alluring than
it was possible to be. Suddenly he shrieked curses at Calhoun. They were horrible to listen to. He screamed—

Calhoun raised the paint-gun, his features twisted and wry.
He sent a single small vortex ring.

In the sudden silence that fell, a tiny, tinny voice sounded
from the spacephone receiver at one side of the laboratory.

"*Calling ground,*" said a voice faintly. "*Ship from home
with passengers calling ground on Maris III. Calling
ground . . .*"

Calhoun jerked his head about and listened to the re-
iterated call. Then he bent to the necessary next thing to
be done with his prisoner.

"*Calling ground,*" said the voice patiently. "*We do not
read you. If you are answering, we do not pick up your
signal. We will go in orbit and continue to call. Calling
ground . . .*"

Calhoun turned it off. Murgatroyd said inquiringly:
"Chee?"

"That's a deadline," said Calhoun grimly. "For us. It's a
shipload of happy, immunized colonists, ready to land here.
We blew the landing grid, Murgatroyd, when they tried to
butter us over the inside of the Med Ship. Apparently we

blew their spacephone at the same time. So the spacephone in this ship, here is the only one working. And we have too much sense to answer that call. But it gives us a deadline, just the same. If they still don't raise their friends, the ship may stay in orbit, but somebody'll come down in a lifeboat to find out what's wrong. And that will shoot the works! We'll have a passenger ship full of enthusiasts ready to land and finish the mopping-up business—and us! There's just you and me, Murgatroyd, to take care of the situation. Let's get at it!"

But it was very close to dawn when he and Murgatroyd left the grounded ship. Calhoun grimaced when he saw the vast crimson glory of approaching sunrise in the sky to the east. He saw a ground-car before the building in which the landing grid controls were housed.

"Worked up like these characters are," said Calhoun, "and suspecting somebody of spreading plagues for them to catch, they won't be cordial to anybody who didn't come here with them. I don't like the idea of trying simply to walk away when there's all this daylight. I think we'd better try to take that car, Murgatroyd. Come along!"

He headed for the control building. Judging by the night before, the occupied rooms had no windows facing toward the landed spacecraft. But he moved cautiously from one great arch-foundation to the next. When he'd reached the last possible bit of shelter, however, the ground-car was still fifty yards away.

"We run for it," he told Murgatroyd.

He and the tiny *tormal* bolted through the rosy dawnlight. They had covered thirty yards when someone came out of the control building. He moved toward the ground-car. He heard Calhoun's pelting footsteps on the turf. He turned. For one instant he stared. Calhoun was a stranger. There should be no living strangers on this planet—they should all be dead. Here was an explanation of two men found unconscious and probably dying, and two more missing. The invader roared. His blaster came out.

Calhoun fired first. The snarling rasp of a blaster is unmistakable. The invader's weapon burst thunderously.

"Run!" snapped Calhoun.

Voices. A man peered out a window. Calhoun was a stranger with a blaster in his hand. The sight of him was a challenge to murder. The man in the window yelled. As Calhoun snapped a shot at him he jerked inside and the window crackled and smoked where the blaster-charge hit.

Man and *tormal* reached the line of the ground-car and the building door. The door was open. Calhoun swung up the dextrethyl sprayer and pumped explosive dextrethyl vapor into the room in a steady stream of vortex rings. He backed toward the ground-car, with Murgatroyd dancing agitatedly about his feet.

There was a crash of glass. Somebody'd plunged out a window. There were rushing feet inside. They'd be racing toward the door, from inside. But the hallway, or whatever was immediately inside, would be filled with anesthetic gas. Men would gasp and fall.

A man did fall. Calhoun heard the crash of his body as it hit the floor. But another man came plunging around the building's corner, blaster out, searching for Calhoun. He had to sight his target though, and then aim for it. Calhoun had only to pull his trigger. He did.

More shouting inside the building. More rushing feet. More falls. Then there was the beginning of the rasping snarl of a blaster, and finally a cushioned, booming, roaring detonation which was the ignited dextrethyl vapor. The blast lifted part of the building's roof. It shattered partitions. It blew out windows.

Calhoun backed toward the ground-car. A blaster-bolt flashed past him. He deliberately traversed the building with his trigger held down. Smoke and flame leaped up. At least one more invader crumpled. Calhoun heard a voice yelling:

"*We're being attacked! The natives are throwing bombs! Rally! Rally! We need help!*"

It would be a broadcast call for assistance. Wherever men idled or loafed or tried desultorily to find something to loot, they would hear it. Even the crew working to repair the landing grid—and they would be close by—would hear it and swarm to help. Hunters would come. Men in cars—

Calhoun snatched Murgatroyd to the seat beside him. He turned the ignition key and tires screamed as he shot away.

Chapter VIII

"It has to be recognized that man is a social animal in the same sense, though in a different manner, that ants and bees are social creatures. For an ant city to prosper, there have to be natural laws to protect it against unfavorable actions on the part of its members. It is not enough to speak of instincts to prevent antisocial actions. There are mutations of instinct as well as of form, in ants as in other creatures. It is not enough even to speak of social pressure, which among ants would be an impulse to destroy deviant members of the community. There are natural laws to protect an ant city against the instinct-control which would destroy it, as well as against the abandonment of instincts or actions necessary to the ant city as a whole. There are, in short, natural laws and natural forces which protect societies against their own members. In human society. . ."

Probability and Human Conduct——Fitzgerald

THE HIGHWAYS were, of course, superb. The car raced forward, and its communicator began to chatter as somebody in the undamaged part of the grid-control building announced hysterically that a stranger had killed men and gotten away in a car. It described its course. It commanded that he be headed off. It shrilly demanded that he be killed, killed, killed!

Another voice took over. This voice was curt and coldly furious. It snapped precise instructions.

And Calhoun found himself on a gracefully curving, rising road. It soared, and he was midway between towers when another car flashed toward him. He took his blaster in his left hand. In the spilt second during which the cars passed each other, he blasted it. There was a monstrous surge of smoke and flame as the stricken car's Duhanne cell shorted and vaporized half the metal of the car itself.

There came other voices. Somebody had sighted the explosion. The voice in the communicator roared for silence. *"You,"* he rasped. *"If you got him, report yourself!"*

"Chee-chee-chee!" chattered Murgatroyd excitedly.

But Calhoun did not report.

"He got one of us," raged the icy voice. *"Get ahead of him and blast him!"*

Calhoun's car went streaking down the far side of the traffic bridge. It rounded a curve on two wheels. It flashed between two gigantic empty buildings and came to a side road, and plunged into that, and came again to a division and took the left-hand turn, and next time took the right. But the muttering voices continued in the communicator. One of the invaders was ordered to the highest possible bridge from which he could watch all lower-level roadways. Others were to post themselves here and there—and to stay still! A group of four cars was coming out of the storage building. Blast any single car in motion. Blast it! And report, report, report!

"I suspect," said Calhoun to the agitated Murgatroyd beside him, "that this is what is known as military tactics. If they ring us in . . . There aren't but so many of them, though. The trick for us is to get out of the city. We need more choices for action. So—"

The communicator panted a report of his sighting, from a cobweblike bridge at he highest point of the city. He was heading—

He changed his heading. He had so far seen but one of his pursuers' cars. Now he went racing along empty, curving highways, among untenanted towers and between balconied walls with blank-eyed windows gazing at him everywhere.

It was nightmarish because of the magnificence and the emptiness of the city all about him. He plunged along graceful highways, across delicately arched bridges, through crazy ramifications of its lesser traffic arteries—and he saw no motion anywhere. The wind whistled past the car windows, and the tires sang a high-pitched whine, and the sun shone down and small clouds floated tranquilly in the sky. There were no signs of life or danger anywhere on the splendid highways or in the beautiful buildings. Only voices muttered in the communicator of the car. He'd been seen here, flashing around a steeply banked curve. He'd swerved from a waiting ambush by pure chance. He'd—

He saw green to the left. He dived down a sloping ramp toward one of the smaller park-areas of the city.

And as he came from between the stone guard-rails of the road, the top of the car exploded over his head. He swerved and roared into dense shrubbery, jerked Murgatroyd free despite the *tormal's* clinging fast with all four paws and his tail, and dived into the underbrush. Somehow, instinctively, he clung to the vortex-gun.

He ran, with his free hand plucking solidified droplets of hot metal from his garments and his flesh. They hurt abominably. But the man who'd fired wouldn't believe he'd missed, followed as his blasting was by the instant wrecking of the car. That man would report success before he moved in to view the corpse of his supposed victim. But there'd be other cars coming. At the moment it was necessary for Calhoun to get elsewhere, fast.

He heard the rushing sound of arriving cars while he panted and sweated through the foliage of the park. He reached the far side and a road, and on beyond there was a low stone wall. He knew instantly what it was. Service highways ran in cuts, for the most part roofed over to hide them from sight, but now and again open to the sky for ventilation. He'd entered the city by one of them. Here was another. He swung himself over the wall and dropped. Murgatroyd recklessly and excitedly followed.

It was a long drop, and he staggered when he landed. He heard a soft rushing noise above. A car raced past. Instants later, another.

Limping, Calhoun ran to the nearest service gate. He entered and closed it. Scorched and aching, he climbed to the echoing upper stories of this building. Presently he looked out. His car had been wrecked in one of the smaller park-areas of the city. Now there were other cars at two-hundred-yard intervals all about it. It was believed that he was in the brushwood somewhere. Besides the cars of the cordon, there were now twenty men on foot receiving orders from an authoritative figure in their midst.

They scattered. Twenty yards apart, they began to move across the park. Other men arrived and strengthened the cordon toward which he was supposed to be driven. A fly could not have escaped.

Those who marched across the park began methodically to burn it to ashes before them with their blasters.

Calhoun watched. Then he remembered something and was appalled. Two days before while he was among the fugitives in the glade, Kim Walpole had asked hungrily if they whose lives he had saved could not do something to help him. And he'd said that if they saw the smoke of a good-sized fire in the city they might investigate. He'd had not the faintest intention of calling on them. But they might see this cloud of smoke and believe he wanted them to come and help!

"Damn!" he said wryly to Murgatroyd. "After all, there's a limit to any one series of actions with probable favorable chance consequences. I'd better start a new one. We might have whittled the invaders down and made the rest run away, but I had to start using a car! And that led to the chance making of a fire! So now we start all over with a new policy."

He explored the building quickly. He prepared his measures. He went back to the window from which he'd looked. He cracked it open.

He opened fire with his blaster. The range was long, but with the beam cut down to minimum spread he'd knocked over a satisfying number of the men below before they swarmed toward the building, sending before them a barrage of blaster-fire that shattered the windows and had the stone facade smoking furiously.

"This," said Calhoun, "is an occasion where we have to change their advantage in numbers and weapons into an unfavorable circumstance for them. They'll be brave because they're many. L 's go!"

He met four ground-car loads of refugees with his arms

in the air. He did not want to be shot down by mistake. He said hurriedly, when Kim and the other lean survivors gathered about him:

"Everything's all right. We've a pack of prisoners but we won't bother to feed them intravenously for the moment. How'd you get the ground-cars?"

"Hunters," said Kim savagely. "We found them and killed them and took their cars. We found some other refugees, too, and I cured them—at least they will be cured soon. When we saw the smoke, we started for the city. Some of us still have the plague, but we've all had our serum shots. And half of us have arms now."

"All of us have arms," said Calhoun, "and to spare. The invaders are quite peacefully sleeping—just about all of them. I did knock over a few with long-range blaster-shots, and they won't wake up. Most of them, though, tried to storm a building from which I'd fired on them. I stood them off a fair length of time, and then ducked after dumping dextrethyl in the air-conditioning system. Murgatroyd and I waited a suitable time and then lengthened their slumber period with polysulphate. I doubt there'll be any more trouble with the butchers. But we've got to get to the spaceship they landed in. I fixed it so it couldn't possibly take off, but there are some calls coming in from space. The only working spacephone here is in the ship. The first load of immunized, enthusiastic colonists are in orbit now, giving the gang aground a little more time to answer. I want you people to talk to them."

"We'll bring their ship down," said the broad-bearded man hungrily, "and blast them as they come out of the port!"

Calhoun shook his head.

"To the contrary," he said mildly. "You'll put on the clothes of some of our prisoners, and you'll let yourselves be seen by the joyous newcomers in their spacephone screen. You'll pretend to be the characters we really have safely sleeping, and you'll say that the plague worked much too well. You'll say it wiped out the original inhabitants—that's you—and then changed into a dozen other plagues and wiped out all the little butcher-boys who came to mop up. You'll give details of the other kinds of plague that the real plague turned into. You'll be pathetic. You'll beg them to land and pick up you four or five dying, multiply diseased, highly contagious survivors. You'll tell them the plague has mutated until even the native animals are dying of it. Flying things fall dead from the air. Chirping things in the trees and grass are wiped out. You'll picture Maris III as a world on which no animal life can hope ever to live again,—and you'll beg them to come down and pick you up and take you home with them."

The broad-bearded man stared. Then he said, "But they won't land."

"No," agreed Calhoun. "They won't. They'll go home. Unless the government has them all killed before they can talk, they'll tell their world what happened. They'll be half-dead with fear that the immunizing shots they received will mutate and turn them into the kind of plague victims you'll make yourself look like. And just what do you think will happen on the world they came from?"

Kim said hungrily, "They'll kill their rulers. They'll try to to do it before they die of the plagues they'll imagine. They'll revolt! If a man has a belly-ache he'll go crazy with terror and try to kill a government official because his government has murdered him!"

Kim drew a deep breath. He smiled with no amusement at all.

"I like that," he said with a sort of deadly calm. "I like that very much."

"After all," observed Calhoun, "once an empire had been started, with the subjugated populations kept subdued by a threat of plague, how long would it be before the original population was enslaved by the same threat? Go and invent some interesting plagues and make yourselves look terrifying. Heaven knows you're lean enough! But you can make yourselves look worse. I said, once, that a medical man sometimes has to use psychology in addition to the regular measures against plague. The Med Service will check on that planet presently, but I think its ambition to be a health hazard to the rest of the galaxy will be ended."

"Yes," said Kim. He moved away. Then he stopped. "What about your prisoners? They're knocked out now. What about them?"

Calhoun shrugged.

"Oh, we'll let them sleep until we finish repairing the landing grid. I think I can be helpful with that."

"Every one of them is a murderer," growled the broad-bearded man.

"True," agreed Calhoun. "But lynching is bad business. It even offers the possibility of unfavorable chance consequences. Let's take care of the shipload of colonists first."

So they did. It was odd how they could take a sort of pleasure in the enactment of imagined disaster even greater than they had suffered. Their eyes gleamed happily as they went about their task.

The passenger ship went away. It did not have a pleasant journey. When it landed, its passengers burst tumultuously out of the spaceport and told their story. Their home world went into a panic which was the more uncontrollable because the people had been very carefully told how deadly the tamed plagues would be to the inhabitants of worlds that they might want to take over. But now they believed the tamed plagues had turned upon them.

The deaths, especially among members of the ruling class, were approximately equal in number to those a deadly pandemic would have caused.

But back on Maris III things moved smoothly. Rather more than eighty people, altogether, were found and treated and ultimately helped with the matter of the slumbering invaders. That was almost a labor of love. Certainly it gave great satisfaction. The landing grid was back in operation two days after the passenger ship left. They took the landed spaceship and smashed its drive and communicators, and they wrecked its Duhanne cells. They took out the breech-plugs of the rockets and dumped the rocket fuel, saving just enough for the little Med Ship. Naturally, they removed the lifeboats.

And then they revived the unconscious butcher-invaders and put them, one by one, into the spacecraft in which they had come. That craft was now a hulk. It could not drive or use rockets or even signal. Its vision screens were blind; the Med Ship used some of them.

And then they used the landing grid—Calhoun checking the figures—and they put their prisoners up in orbit to await the arrival of proper authority. They could feed themselves, but any attempt at escape would be pure and simple suicide. They could not attempt to escape.

"And now," said Calhoun, when the planet was clean of strangers again, "now I'll bring my ship to the grid. We'll recharge my Duhanne cells and replace my vision screens. I can make it here on rockets, but it's a long way to headquarters. So I'll report, and a field team will come here and check out the planet, artificial plagues included. They'll arrange, somehow, to take care of the prisoners up in orbit. That's not my affair. Maybe Dettra Two would like to have them. In the meantime, they can search their consciences."

Kim said, frowning:

"You put something over on us! You kept us so busy we forgot one man. You said there'd be a microbiologist in the invaders' party. You said he'd probably be the man who had invented the plague. And he's up there in orbit with the rest—he'll get no more than they get! You put something over on us. He deserves some special treatment!"

Calhoun said very evenly:

"Revenge is always apt to have unfavorable chance consequences. Let him alone. You've no right to punish him. You've only the right to punish a child to correct it, or to punish a man to deter others from doing what he's done. Do you expect to correct the kind of man who'd invent the plague that flourished here, and meant to use it for the making of an empire of slaves? Do you think others need to be deterred from trying the same thing?"

Kim said thickly:

"But he's a murderer! All the murders were his! He deserves—"

"Condign punishment?" asked Calhoun sharply. "You've no right to administer it. Anyhow, think what he's up against!"

"He's—he's . . ." Kim's face changed. "He's up there in orbit, hopeless, with his butchers all around him and blaming

him for the fix they're in. They've nothing to do but hate
him. Nothing . . ."

"You didn't arrange that situation," said Calhoun coldly.
"He did. You simply put prisoners in a safe place because
it would be impractical to guard them, otherwise. I suggest
you forget him."

Kim looked sickish. He shook his head to clear it. He tried
to thrust the man who'd planned pure horror out of his mind.
He said slowly:

"I wish we could do something for you."

"Put up a statue," said Calhoun dryly, "and in twenty
years nobody will know what it was for. You and Helen are
going to be married, aren't you?" When Kim nodded, Calhoun
said, "In course of time, if you remember and think it worthwhile, you may inflict a child with my name. That child will
wonder why, and ask, and so my memory will be kept green
for a full generation."

"Longer than that," insisted Kim. "You'll never be forgotten
here!"

Calhoun grinned at him.

Three days later, which was six days longer than he'd
expected to be aground on Maris III, the landing grid heaved
the little Med Ship out to space. The beautiful, nearly empty
city dwindled as the grid field took the tiny spacecraft out
to five planetary diameters and there released it. And Calhoun spun the Med Ship about and oriented it carefully for
that place in the Cetis cluster where Med Service Headquarters was. He threw the overdrive switch.

The universe reeled. Calhoun's stomach seemed to turn
over twice, and he had a sickish feeling of spiraling dizzily
in what was somehow a cone. He swallowed. Murgatroyd
made gulping noises. There was no longer a universe per-
ceptible about the ship. There was dead silence. Then those
small random noises began which have to be provided if a
man is not to crack up in the dead stillness of a ship traveling
at thirty times the speed of light.

Then there was nothing more to do. In overdrive travel
there is never anything to do but pass the time away.

Murgatroyd took his right-hand whiskers in his right paw and licked them elaborately. He did the same to his left-hand whiskers. He contemplated the cabin, deciding upon a soft place in which to go to sleep.

"Murgatroyd," said Calhoun severely, "I have to have an argument with you. You imitate us humans too much! Kim Walpole caught you prowling around with an injector, starting to give our prisoners another shot of polysulfate. It might have killed them! Personally, I think it would have been a good idea, but in a medical man it would have been most unethical. We professional men have to curb our impulses! Understand?"

"*Chee!*" said Murgatroyd. He curled up and wrapped his tail meticulously about his nose, preparing to doze.

Calhoun settled himself comfortably in his bunk. He picked up a book. It was Fitzgerald on *Probability and Human Conduct.*

He began to read as the ship went on through emptiness.

www.ingramcontent.com/pod-product-compliance
Lightning Source LLC
Chambersburg PA
CBHW020730250626

47155CB00006B/2239